Croyd—

Chairman of Sol Galaxy, he is an immortal and a time traveler, a master of telepathy and teleportation.

Dino Trigg—

Charismatic First Minister of Sol Galaxy and beloved protégé of Croyd, Dino has developed a powerful system of psychophysical forces with which he can project his will upon others.

MEGALOMANIA is the remarkable story of these two godlike beings—and of the struggle that ensues when Trigg, failing to oust Croyd from the Chairmanship of Sol Galaxy, launches a cosmic vendetta against him. . . .

Novels by Ian Wallace

HELLER'S LEAP
THE LUCIFER COMET
THE RAPE OF THE SUN
A VOYAGE TO DARI
THE WORLD ASUNDER
Z-STING
MEGALOMANIA

MEGALOMANIA

IAN WALLACE

DAW BOOKS, INC.

DONALD A. WOLLHEIM, PUBLISHER

1633 Broadway, New York, NY 10019

First Printing, May 1989
1 2 3 4 5 6 7 8 9
Printed in the U.S.A.

ONE MORE FOR MY LIB

who is not in this book
nor, this time, anywhere else

Radiant with love for all people she meets;
    loved in return by all people who know her.
Good God above! when it snows, rains, or sleets.
    let balmy breezes be all that you blow her!

. . . Raised impious war in Heaven and battle proud,
With vain attempt. Him the Almighty Power
Hurled headlong flaming from the ethereal sky,
With hideous ruin and combustion, down
To bottomless perdition . . .

* * *

. . . Thither, full fraught with mischievous revenge,
Accurst, and in a cursed hour, he hies.

—John Milton,
Paradise Lost

The Action

CAPER FOUR
CLIMAX FOR
THE JET-MASTER 127

CAPER ULTIMA
REALITY-FACING 155

Author's Forenote

MEGALOMANIA constitutes another episode in Croyd's epic operations to defeat forces of evil in and near Sol Galaxy (the locus of the planet Erth which is not *our* Earth but is so much like it that the reader can feel at home there).

The protagonist—the villain—is Dino Trigg, a galactically high-ranking protégé of Croyd, who rebels against his fathering friend and, frustrated in his drive for power, resorts to a revenge that is nothing short of cosmic. *And he can do it.*

The mindsoul of Dino is obviously abnormal. However, he is not technically insane; he is thoroughly in touch with reality, as at one point he makes clear to Captain Kedrin.

Galactic jets are real. The specific jets which are cited in the story, other than the herein-created jet out of the Magellanic Clouds, exist, and they exhibit the ferocious lengths and energy-levels herein cited.

If here and there a reader seems to perceive allusions to the ejection from paradise of the Archangel Lucifer and to the Old Faust story, that is the reader's honored privilege.

—IAN WALLACE
Western North Carolina, 1988

CAPER ONE

REBELLION IN HEAVEN

1. The Rebellion

Parked in Nereid's orbit around Neptune, taffy-haired Kolly Kedrin took advantage of her captaincy by occupying the best chair on the President's Bridge in order to use its incomparable holotelly during election or reelection of a Galactic chairman (the incumbent being Croyd). She'd be alone in there; her first and second officers had shore leave, and the rest of her crew including her command android had their own information-input facilities.

History was about to be made, and Kolly by God would select and control her own angles for it. Occupying all of the cycloramically curved bulkhead bridge-wall, the screen responded holistically to any holographic telecast such as this one—which in effect meant that a watcher could prowl the scene at will, alternately in front of the action or behind it or in it.

Because the year was 2513, the directing board of Galactic, Ltd., tops among all governmental corporations, was meeting to determine by vote whether Board Chairman and Chief Executive Croyd should, during another half-decade, continue to govern Sol Galaxy whose most prosperous planet was Erth. Normally, Chairman Croyd would preside over board meetings; but at this quintennial election, with Croyd standing for reelection, it was the President of the Interplanetary Union who occupied the chair, the Union being the employer of Galactic.

President Tannen was a benign but decisive and endlessly knowledgeable, semi-corpulent white-haired Sinite out of Erth's Gaza Strip. His age was crowding eighty. He had been elected Interplanetary President, repeatedly, by majorities of all the affiliated planetary governments in Sol Galaxy: the democratic or authoritarian republics of fifty-four planets in fifty-two planetary systems. Tannen hired and could fire a governmental corporation to rule the galaxy; he kept hiring Galactic, Ltd., which had ruled since 2475, under Croyd's top leadership since 2496. Tannen could not fire Croyd without firing the whole corporation.

These arrangements made Croyd the most powerful person in the galaxy. And because Croyd was Croyd, Tannen was delighted to have it so. During his long life, never had Tannen known a man who so remarkably blended into his leadership wisdom, psycho-physical agility, personal charm, and interpersonal caring.

Action in the board room: people entering. Kolly straightened with interest; whereafter she settled back, with a container of popcorn and a soft beverage on her chair arm near the remote controls, to watch the proceedings studiously and yet with stirrings of excitement. Had not Dino Trigg promised her astonishment?

The austerely functional board room was ovoid. Seated people were arranged along both side walls, one parenthesis open-facing the other. Between them, a broad space of floor was empty; but by crouching and peering upward, Kolly could see a large device hanging above and presumably lowerable.

Chairman Croyd was seated behind a small desk at the center of one parenthesis of small desks facing the board. He was flanked by the ten ministers who were his top officers in Galactic.

Trigg sat at Croyd's immediate right, being first among these ministers. Kolly was intently aware of Croyd's involuntarily magnetic appearance—his auburn hair verging on flame, his eyes as blue as the octopus-haunted Blue Grotto, his ineffable effluvium of inward substance. His evident age was a wiry-muscular loose-athletic thirty-six—after (her backgrounding apprehended) nearly forty years of being thirty-six inside and out. (Kolly didn't know about his prior centuries.)

But in view of how intimately she had begun to know him, Kolly was shiveringly aware of Dino Trigg's charisma. He was smilingly relaxed at the moment, but poised for electrical deployment. (For seated-next-to-him Croyd, there was nothing new about that smilingly electrical charm; Croyd, however—being in bodily proximity—sensed a great deal that was abnormally more, and Croyd prickled with apprehension.)

Croyd and his battery of ministers were gazing somewhat upward at a toward-them-open, daised counter-parenthesis: a broad semicircular highly-polished ebonoid table behind whose convex edge were nine swiveling easy chairs, eight of which were occupied (Croyd having vacated his own center chair for this quintennial occasion). High above each of the chairs hovered a lowerable crystal cube which, at meetings where some board member could not be physically present because of extra-planetary business (boondoggling or honest), would descend to display the image of that member: the image would be able to hear, speak, and vote. All, however, were physically on hand today: the cubes were dark.

Behind and above the board-arc sat President Tannen; behind and above Tannen was positioned SECYCOM which did not count as human.

Tannen had appointed Croyd as Temporary Chairman in 2496, a year when Croyd's predecessor had been disabled by a mind-attack from the Greater Magellanic Cloud. Croyd had defeated the attack. Reelected, he continued to call himself Temporary Chairman on the reasonable ground that there was no such thing as a five-year permanency. In 2507, he had resigned, accepting a transient embassy to milliparsecs-distant Djinn Galaxy. In 2509, his successor as chairman had come up dead. At Tannen's i-radio urging, Croyd had returned, again as chairman, to quell a couple of planetary threats.

Now, in 2513, Croyd felt uncomfortable here, having been privately advised by Tannen that Dino in secret had been hard-lobbying for his own election.

Croyd had brought Dino cherishingly along and, returning to power, had elevated Dino from Minister of Sciences and Arts to First Minister. Dino had always been an exuberant blend of intellectuality and gallantry, driving his life as he drove his space-scouter: perceptively and with accurate precalculation of risks. He had always practiced devoted loyalty to Croyd, his fosterfather.

In Dino's warmly grateful presence, Croyd had several times intimated to Tannen and to board members that apparently Trigg would be the best of all possible chairmen by the time of Croyd's anticipated *final* retirement in 2518. But now Dino was about to demonstrate that a five-year wait would be, for him, a bit much.

Tannen contemplated Trigg. Kolly contemplated both men. Incumbent Croyd was choosing not to glance at his magnificently naughty protégé; Croyd was watching his own hands folded on his desk, and the fingers of those hands were quiescent. Silently, in his own way, Dino was praying—which is to say, he was upstirring the mystical depths of himself.

Tannen spoke now, easily although he was feeling unease. "Hearing no objection, I will proceed to the prime business. Chairman Croyd, are you standing for reelection?" Croyd stood, assented, sat. "Prior to discussion by this board, do you wish to enter any remarks?" Croyd replied, holding his middle-baritone voice in restraint: "Not prior to discussion, sir."

Tannen queried: "Does anyone wish to arise as a competing candidate for the chair?"

Dino Trigg stood: hair and trim beard golden blond, eyes a surprising dark brown, handsome-flexible-potent. His generally unexpected self-presentation startled and even shocked his fellow ministers and some board members.

Inquired unrufflable Tannen: "First Minister Trigg, you are challenging Chairman Croyd for the chair of this board?"

"I am, sir." Dino engaged the eyes of Tannen directly.

Unsurprised but hurt, Croyd studied the faces of his eight board members, but he could descry nothing as to their voting intentions. (With respect to six of the members, Dino knew.)

Equably Tannen told the challenger: "Sir, we have known you during some years as a remarkably fine administrator. We are also aware of your researches and achievements in astrophysics, in spatiotemporal analysis, and in psychosociology. Unless a member of this board objects, these remarks about your record will be stipulated—which will save you the embarrassment of hornblowing and allow you to go immediately into the meat of your challenge." Tannen looked about him. "Hearing no objection, I so stipulate." SECYCOM emitted one confirming beep.

Tannen proceeded: "Now, sir, please give us any reasons why we should prefer you to Croyd as chairman."

Deep within him, Dino could virtually *hear* the lyric tenor of his friendly resident demon: *Right here, Dino, restraint, restraint.*

Dino began: "Mister President, I do feel that I should begin by adding a word or two about my experiential qualifications for the chair. Be it recalled that there have been long periods of time when Chairman Croyd, my revered friend and mentor, has absented himself from his post, making it necessary for his deputy to act in his stead. Temporal analysis shows that during Croyd's fifteen years in the chair, not counting the 2507-9 hiatus, his deputies, including myself during the past three years, have governed this galaxy more than sixty percent of the time; in my own case, it has been sixty-three percent. I have reminded you of these circumstances only to make it clear that I can handle the job. However, more affirmatively—"

The inward tenor: *Great, Dino! unfair, unfair, great! But now—let it roll!* And this time, Croyd actually mind-heard the mind-voice; he hadn't meant to mind-spy, which he greatly disliked doing, but his hintermind had inadvertently probed, and his mental eyebrows arched high.

Dino: "Mr. President, have I the board's leave to present some pertinent visuals?"

Having looked back and forth at the board members and forward at Croyd to detect negation signals which, however, were not forthcoming, Tannen assented to the visuals. Dino spoke directly to SECYCOM, issuing instructions which caused that robot to lower the overhead object—which turned out, of course, to be a crystal holosphere four meters in diameter, swinging gently a meter above the floor and nearly filling the inside of the desk/ table parentheses—causing board members and ministers to lean far back in their adjustable chairs in order for their eyes to focus comfortably on sphere-heart. SECYCOM had darkened the room, filling it with pale blue twilight.

After a suitable pause for dramatic impact, they heard the first minister's quiet, command-easy voice: "Roll Exhibit A." If internally he was going nuclear-critical, nevertheless he stayed all quiet command-com in his externality.)

The results of his order were enchanting, even though they were familiar stuff to most of the watchers, including Kolly. The holosphere melted into black space filled with varihued stars, with a particularly bright star near center. The watchers zoomed in on that star-seeming: it became a nebula, then took discernible form as an elliptical galaxy which approached them until it filled the tube.

"Deep-tint the tube and keep rolling," Dino commanded; and the nebula dimmed and began to recede; at the same time, the galaxy appeared to rotate out of its plane until it was edge-on, presumably (if this was not animation) because of a repositioning of the camera-ships. "Hold the roll," he directed; and then he turned to the board:

"Mister President and honorable board members, let me caution you: even with the holotube in deep tint, the brightnesses that you are about to see may exceed the limit of your visual tolerance; this may be true even if your lens implants adapt to light. I do urge that, at least for the moment, you squint to exclude some of the light." He swiveled 180 degrees: "Fellow Galactic ministers, the same applies to you, of course; and" (he looked upward) "it applies even to our telewatchers everywhere in the galaxy, unless they now darken their tubes almost to minimum brightness."

In the board room, his audience stiffened, and some donned dark glasses. Aboard her ship, Kolly shrugged and watched; her doubly indirect tube-image ought to be sufficiently dimmed in transmission.

Returning his attention to SECYCOM, Dino told it: "Resume rolling."

Several cries of distress were heard when a multicolored flame-serpent flared into light-life that hissed out beyond the tube curvature to convert the room's dimness into stroboscopic hyperdaylight; so might the post-medieval twentieth-century physicists and reporters have staggered screaming back, flinging forearms across eyes, when the first of all nuclear fireballs on Erth blindingly ignited itself.

Moments later, grace to one or another sort of eye guard, the jet-spumes resolved themselves into describable form and color even for momentarily blinded and soul-affrighted Kolly who promptly, after all, darkened her picture and looked elsewhere until the after images paled and died. When she returned to the screen, the full images of two mirror-symmetrical plumes in fiery varicolor had achieved ultradynamic definition.

As an interglactic spacer, of course Kolly knew what the plume-flares were, even while Dino was explaining them to his board. (Croyd, she noticed, was resting his forehead on his folded hands and was frowning down.) She and they were viewing the violent dual ejaculations of an elliptical galaxy astronomically known as 3C-449 and also, by spacers and by irreverent astronomers, as Hapi the Bull because of these twin fire jets which fancifully resembled bull horns (not the vocal but rather the prickery sort): curving gently upward from galactic center, then sharply downward, then terminally upward, each horn being tipped by a hot-spot inferno. You couldn't see these fire-horns at all with raw human vision even at normal radio-telescope frequencies; but nowadays every deep-space ship such as Kolly's *Sterbenräuber* was equipped with transcolor visiscreens which opened up the higher wavelength ranges. Ironically, *Sterbenräuber*'s transcolor equipment was unnecessary now, because in Kolly's tube-picture Dino had already evoked transcolor in the demonic holograph that he was exhibiting on Nereid to his board members.

He was commenting quietly, suavely (while puzzled and alarmed Croyd mind-felt the heat of his inward arousal): "I am of course exhibiting the jet-spumes out of the galaxy called 3C-449 which is an inconvenient hundred million light-years away from us. Each of those jets is about two hundred thousand light-years in length. Each jet terminates in a hot-spot lobe in which the dammed-up energy is equal to that of a quarter of a million suns such as our Sol.

"Ours is indeed a complex universe. Numerous galaxies eject such jets. They may attain lengths of a million light-years—I said a *million* light-years, that is, more than three hundred thousand parsecs, many times the diameter of our magnificent galaxy—with hot-spot lobes deploying the energy of ten million suns.

"That much energy. I said, honored board-members—and how fully aware I am that most of you deploy Erth-vital industrial operations which are ravenous for new energy sources—I said: that much *energy!*"

The responding board-sigh was like the soughing of a thrilled breeze.

"They constitute," Dino asserted, "a natural resource that wastes itself unharvested.

"As chairman, I will be their harvester. Our galaxy will feast on the harvest."

Croyd (but not Kolly) noticed that, while Tannen and two board members were leaning forward, six board members were sitting back relaxed and smug. Four of the six were women; one was a man; the sex of the sixth was ambiguous. An unsavory hypothesis began to form in Croyd's mind. . . .

"To help you grasp the practicality of my concept," Dino pressed, "I'll remind you that the principle of ultrahigh-efficiency transmittal of a star's energy to one of its planets was established long ago when satellites were dispatched to collect solar energy while orbiting Sol at a ten-million-kilometer radius, transmitting the energy to Erth via mirrors and lasers. With respect to radiant jet-space, we—I, in fact—have recently improved on such primitive methods. Let me show you an instance."

The hologram changed: now it was a single jet rather than a duo, out of a source which Dino lost no time in explaining. "You are looking at a little fellow which does not emanate from a galaxy; instead, it is one of a number of jets within our own galaxy, X-27Q, spewed out by a binary star. We are viewing it from a locus much closer in than in the case of 3C-449, so that in our picture it appears almost equally impressive and chromatic. Now, *this* jet is only a shade over four *hundred* light-years from Sol: easily ready to hand. This relative nearness makes X-27Q an ideal subject for experimentation with energy harvesting, even though its relatively small size makes the potential return low when measured against the necessary investment."

While Croyd's ethos blocked him from telepathically examining Dino's thoughts, it was becoming imperative for the chairman to taste Dino's emotionality. And it was high, high, fiery high; never in Croyd's experience of him had Dino been on such a wild roll! Yet the first minister's delivery demeanor was quietly-persuasively measured. For the first time, Croyd knew an eerie sense of psychic disjuncture between Dino's cognitively governed behavior and Dino's connatively *ungoverned* arousal. . . .

His protégé-competitor was weaving his expert way into a climax. "Honorable board members, please hear this: *we are in fact now* reaping energy from the jet-spume of X-27Q, because of an initiative by your first minister." Croyd was frowning: he had given the nod to Dino's proposal about this; now why would his dear friend use it against him?

Dino was pressing on with it. "We are engineering this research with robot ships which fly into the stem of the jet and implant forcefield turbines therein. Largely to ease the conscience-pain visible in the face of my revered mentor Croyd, I will insert that all, or virtually all, of the energy we thus harvest is being banked for the eventual use of the single human-inhabited planet orbiting X-27Q—a planet whose technology has not yet reached a level where it can make use of such energy at present. But my point is, that the technique is working and is indefinitely extensible— and, as my dear friend Croyd will have to admit, was devised and proposed and experimentally implemented by me and not by him."

Ignoring Croyd's massive wince, Dino sizzled into coda. "Should this board accord me the chair of Galactic, I would prosecute, as my highest creative priority, the extension of this method to major galactic jets such as the pair out of 3C-449 which you first beheld. And that is an approach which Chairman Croyd does not appear even to have thought of. All of us are aware of his inventively lofty creativity during past decades: this I would never discount, I have revered it, I have learned from it. And if, perchance, age has blunted this creativity, never would I cease to revere it as it spurted and molded our galaxy during its time; and if its time should indeed now be done, I pray that everyone in the galaxy will thank his own god for its existence while it existed.

"However, this is 2513—*today*. And I know my duty to this galaxy. As of today—and until such time as I *too* will be sliding into honorable desuetude—I urge that you elect me chairman, for service during my own creative prime."

Dino sat, not looking at Croyd.

Kolly was enthralled at Dino's diabolical audacity. His performance had been distinguished by high virtuosity, and cognitively he was aware of this; his presence had radiated stunning charisma; emotionally (and also rationally, for a certain hidden reason) he knew that he would win. His performance had been intended less to gain new converts than to strengthen and inspire those who were already converted.

Croyd noticed that the two board members who had been leaning forward now appeared concerned and were glancing furtively at Croyd; while the six smug ones remained smug and had eyes only for Trigg. Now Croyd was able to infer which of the board members were in Dino's pocket—and the count for Croyd was not good. Inwardly he kicked himself for fond carelessness: caring for Dino, highly esteeming his protégé's intellectual gifts and energetic self-application and consent-winning charm and (yes!) emotive moderation, Croyd had failed to take account of the molten emotional magma beneath Dino's upward drive. (Or—was the vulcanism in fact something new? sensitive Croyd hadn't previously sensed the degree of it . . .)

One of the board members whose eyes did not seem glazed raised a six-fingered hand. "Mister President, all of us well know about those Croyd-absences, their galaxy-threatening causes, their results which have added up to our galactic survival *not despite but because of* Croyd in the course of his absences."

"Oh, God, yes!" affirmed the second in a deep bell-contralto (although he was male: the vocal quality was a species characteristic). "Not that we weren't fortunate to have Doctor Trigg and prior stellar first ministers on the home front; but I believe that Doctor Trigg, for instance, was discovered and elevated by Croyd; and that during Croyd's more-than-essential absences, Trigg and his predecessors operated in terms of marching orders left behind for them by Croyd."

One of the smug ones sniffed: "Except, it seems, in the matter of the jet-spumes. That, my friends, represented Trigg-initiative and Croyd-ignorance. What *else* has been going on that Croyd has failed to notice?"

Interrupting, the first nonglazed board member launched himself into a solid and detailed report of the Croyd stewardship. The prolix endorsement extended back to Croyd's first appearance on the Galactic scene in 2475, moved through two decades of his service in the Internal Security Ministry (internal to the entire galaxy, that is), and proceeded into his years as chairman (2496-2507, then 2509-2513), not failing to mention what he had accomplished for Dari and Moudjinn in remote Djinn Galaxy during his 2507-09 embassy. This board member included scrutiny of Croyd's longest absences, all on perilous Galactic duty-errands in which Croyd's unique skills had been uniquely pertinent. (*But,* Croyd reminded himself, *most of those skills are no longer uniquely mine, grace to what I have taught my trusted Dino.*) This clear-eyed chipvoiced board member talked for more than twenty minutes; whereafter the clear-eyed contralto affirmed: "I thoroughly concur with my colleague in general and in detail; and each other member among us has always agreed on the indispensable value of Croyd as chairman."

Dino took note that he had failed to convert anybody, but he still had his six who were more than enough. As for Croyd, he winced: should he be truly indispensable—and in his own a priori he could not be that—never would he be able to shake loose from this executive job and get back to creative roving! But when ultimately he would depart, he preferred that his leavetaking be voluntary.

President Tannen: "Further discussion?" The suspect six were zombiesque. It was unlike them, and Dino's charisma alone would never have caused it. Surely Croyd's dearly trusted Trigg had not . . . Well, assume for the argument that Dino for some reason was willing to betray Croyd's trust; still, Dino well knew that projective hypnotism, even should it win him this election, could not hold up permanently; but perhaps he was counting on frequent reinforcement . . .

The man who had contralto-echoed support for Croyd called for the question. Tannen ordered a roll call vote.

Yes, Dino *had* done! And Croyd, in view of his insistent position against mind-invasion without consent by the invaded, comprehended that he was about to be displaced by Dino Trigg who (as Croyd now distressfully understood) harbored no such ethical inhibition, nor any scruple about unfairly attacking his fostering patron.

After a prolonged seventeen seconds of indecision, Croyd's necessary attitude snapped into fix: an unethical man, no matter how ably charismatic he might be, no matter how deeply Croyd might care for him, had no business running a galaxy.

Uninvited, Croyd refused to invade minds or brains—but he could mind-spray a psychic counteragent into the air and see who would inhale it.

Croyd sprayed.

The voting went as follows: "Trigg." "Trigg." "Croyd." "Trigg." "Croyd." "Trigg." "Trigg." "Trigg."

Thanks to Dino, they had confirmed Croyd's belief in his own dispensability, six against two. Dino, having straightened in his chair, turned to confront his mentor Croyd in the radiance of his easy and all-forgiving triumph.

Tannen was querying whether Croyd wished to exercise his voting right; silently, Croyd negated, since his vote apparently would not change the outcome. With reluctance, Tannen prepared to declare Trigg the new Chairman of Galactic, Ltd.

Only, psychic aerosols, once inhaled, require some seconds to take effect; whereafter . . .

A Trigg voter, who had been blinking and headshaking as though she sought to arouse herself from stupor, now blurted: "Mister President, did I vote?" "Aye," said Tannen. "*How* did I vote?" queried the awakening sleeper. Startled, Dino swiveled toward this member who had been a Trigg-certainty. Deadpanned Tannen: "Madam, you voted for Trigg." The member, a normally alert, aggressive tycoon from Centauri, now appeared to be requiring her flaccid mouth to slow-form words: "There has been some mistake, I do not understand; if that was my vote, I wish to change it. Strike my vote for Trigg, and enter my vote for Croyd."

Well, hell, mindsaid Dino's mindguest, *five to three is good enough, you've protected yourself by nailing down more votes than you need; so one of them softened . . .*

A second Trigg voter semi-returned from far away. "Sir, is it possible that I too voted for Trigg?"

Now, wait *a minute . . .*

"You did, sir," Tannen affirmed.

"Mister President, I confess confusion, I am not really prepared to vote at all—"

"Please find and express your vote."

"It has to be that I abstain, I feel incompetent for some reason."

"Are you changing your vote from Trigg to Abstention?"

"If you will, please."

By now, smile gone, Dino was cold and grim. Although Croyd played bland, inwardly his concentration on the developing situation was acute.

Tannen asked SECYCOM for the revised count, which was: Trigg four, Croyd three, one abstention. Again Tannen looked at Croyd, and now the incumbent had to act.

Croyd raised a hand, was recognized, stood, asserted: "Mister President, now I must exercise my right to vote. I vote for Croyd."

He sat, and he pitied Trigg's catatonia while SECYCOM enunciated: "It is tied at four and four with one abstention, and the President is obligated to vote."

"I vote for Croyd!" shot Tannen.

Droned SECYCOM: "Croyd wins, five to four with one abstention."

Tannen clinched it: "Chairman Croyd, you will continue in the chair until the year 2518 ITC, absent something ridiculous. First Minister Trigg, we admire you and we regret your defeat, but you know how it is."

The ambiguously sexed Trigg voter now injected tremulously: "Is it too late for me to change my vote to Croyd?"

Uttering an articulacy, Dino wrenched himself away from behind his desk, stood quivering beside it facing an alarmed board; his anger was cosmic
but

then he chilled
and panicked
and transmuted panic into defiant

flight fury. Pivoting to Croyd, he showed his patron a face whose facile charm had persimmoned into contorted evil. He snarled: "Being waste for all of you, I will waste myself!"

He levitated himself physically above the floor, hovered, roared, midair-jetted out of the board room into the corridor-labyrinth of Nereid. This remarkable behavior was entirely within the Croyd-taught psychophysical capabilities of Dino alone.

(On her feet aboard *Sterbenräuber*, Kolly commanded her telly: "Order Nereid to show you every Trigg pickup!" Nereid could do it, recognizing his emotion-distorted thalamic pattern.)

Charging through corridors with the maddened purpose of a defeated control-and-power-worshiper, Dino bulled his way into Nereid's master support-systems control room, dropped all personnel with sweeping projective hypnosis, shut off Nereid's artificial gravity, deep-breathed during a chancy fifteen seconds, opened an airlock, ran out to the far edge of a ship-launch platform, leg-thrust himself off the edge in a racing dive, and shot tumbling outward into perpetual night among stars, mechanically certain to die swiftly in airless space and eventually to body-ploop into the ambiguous surface of Neptune.

2. Enter the Devil

"Follow Trigg!" Kolly stentored; and since anyhow the cameras in the ship-launch platform on Nereid routinely were following him, *Sterbenräuber*'s Kolly-directed sensors were picking him up (thanks to UHF floodlights) while, smallening, he receded into outer darkness.

Into that darkness he vanished. But Kolly, an on-the-ball captain, had computers on the angle-and-thrust vectors of his departure, measuring his consequent directional velocity against time, taking into account the almost-negligible slowing introduced by occasional sub-atomic particles in the not-quite-total vacuum of deep space.

She hurried to the operational bridge (about five seconds transit), fastened her attention on the computer display, and directed the command robot: "Depart formation and go to the vicinity of where-when he must be. Not too close, we mustn't alarm him, but we may decide to scoop him up."

Sterbenräuber moved out. Properly, Kolly should have checked with Astrofleet authority, but she didn't; and later she would rationalize that First Minister Trigg was the big boss of Astrofleet along with a number of other governmental sectors. As a result of her Trigg-pursuit, she missed immediately subsequent Tannen/Croyd action on Nereid.

* * *

While, thanks to Dino's enraged button pushing, all personnel aboard Nereid floated in wall-to-wall freefall breathlessness, alarmed Croyd rocketed through the Trigg-traversed corridors to the same control room, saw on its telly-monitor Dino pushing off from the launch platform into space, restored all Nereid systems, ran to the launch platform, consulted instruments to obtain the vectors of Dino's thrust and consequent freefall trajectory, pushed off with exactly the same space coordinates but with measurably more leg thrust: natural, unaided, head-naked pursuit of a man by a man in unbreathable space.

Neither Dino nor Croyd had bothered with a life-support suit; the reasons were the same, but the motives were different. Both of them had, prior to push-off, stored oxygen in their muscular tissues: Trigg had been taught the psychophysical trick by Croyd; they could draw upon these stores internally, in the spatial absence of oxygen, during hours; neither would explode although suitless, even though their internal body-pressures were pushing outward against the nonpressure of space, because of an internal-gravity mode which Croyd had thought through and adopted and taught to Trigg. But for Dino, the motive was prolongation of his dying; whereas for Croyd, the motive was immediate rescue.

Traumatically defeated Dino Trigg weltered suitless and semiconscious in a decaying Neptune-orbit closer to Neptune than Nereid's orbit and gradually drifting inward-downward. Wanting to die, he was unable to summon death decisively; nevertheless, he knew that when his oxygen store would be exhausted, he would die in space long before Neptune could haul him in; and then, perhaps, Croyd and his board members would comprehend the tragedy of their collective loss . . .

An ultrasonic beam shocked him alert. It was an iradar beam, they were searching for him; they would probably find him, too, because his orbit was calculable with small error from the probable thrust of his legs; the searchers would pull him in, he would live . . . NO! Teleporting in panic, Dino inserted himself into stationary Neptune-orbit more distant from Nereid, at the same time departing present germinality for an uptime locus three days into the past. Croyd had developed both tricks and had taught Dino both tricks, and therefore Dino resented having to deploy them; but they left him spacetime-floating in safety from Croyd and therefore sure to die— whereafter it wouldn't matter, would it?

Closing eyes, he imagined that his body was undulating in space-fluid. He would die when the oxygen would be gone. Nobly he had tried, and nobly he had failed; therefore, this was a species of noble hara-kiri without the traditional gut-mess and unaided by anybody with a samurai sword: suicide all his own, the ultimate nobility

                                                      although it was beginning to fret Dino that his handsome terminal gesture was taking so very long to bring off. Should he perhaps expedite it? How could he try? Expel all the oxygen from his butt? fart lethally? ha! only, he didn't have a method for doing this, other than letting his metabolism prolongedly absorb the oxygen. That accursed-benevolent Croyd had developed gambits only for survival, none for self-destruction—nor, now Dino thought about it, for destruction of others either: only for their neutralization, if they were evil

                              as perhaps Dino was evil

                                        but if he was evil, then evil was good, for he was good, surely he was good—was he not?

Could Dino *will* himself to die? Now, *that* would be a thing which Croyd had never brought off. Dino set himself to try it—and thrust the attempt away, fearing the try, denying the fear, seeking rationale for the denial. His attempt had, however, accelerated his heartbeat, and this in itself was accelerating his death by asphyxiation. New panic! but he required himself to grow calm, he forced himself to *allow* himself to grow calm. Tranquilly now he luxuriated in the depressive serenity of impending spacetime death . . .

Something in his hindmind was raising a vague question. He tried to descry it. The nature of the question was like, now wait just a minute, this is not like me, none of this rebellion against Croyd has been like me, this—*suicide?*—good God, *none of this emotional extravagance is like me . . .*

DINO? The remote mind-cry shocked him into alertness. It denoted Croyd coming in at the wrong moment, and *that* was distinctively unlike Croyd. But there was no way for Croyd to know that in his rescue attempt, he was shortcircuiting Dino's beginnings of self-realization.

Dino waited, listening, comprehending that Croyd's call had to be a mind-call because sounds carry only in atmosphere.

Into his mind came continuation of the Croydcast: *I feel your mind now, my dear friend, so strongly that I know I must be close to you. So you may as well respond.*

An inward hot swelling of angry hostility vaporized Dino's realization-start. Deliberately Dino made his mind-reply mind-feeble. *How you may have found me, Croyd, is a matter of less interest than the trouble you took to look for me. So now you have found me; that is your little triumph. Forget me, Croyd. I sought to dislodge and replace you, I blew it, I am dying by my own decision: forgive me, Croyd; go do what you do.*

Dino, you are throwing away three most precious commodities: your life, your superb mind, your honor. In the most literal sense, I suggest that something has got into you; and I do beg you to face this realistic possibility and let me know what you think—

Desperate Dino-outcry: *Croyd, for the sake of any god, LET GO!*

Pause; then Croyd: *I respect your wish, my friend; I will let go. But if ever you should choose to initiate new contact—just whistle. Do you know how to whistle, Dino?"*

Mind-silence.

The unexpected telepathic exchange with Croyd had partially disengaged Dino from his death-purpose. He was being enlarged by an ineffable sense of what is human yet more than human: of two universals reaching out to each other, one calling and accepting, the other yearning yet bitterly rejecting; of a father letting his son go (as ultimately every father must do) in order to keep his son from spiritually dying.

Repugnantly, Dino thrust himself back into his death-subjectivity. Good, he was free, he would die. Already he was feeling a faint discomfort which meant that his muscle-oxygen was running low. So now he would die, and they would all be sorry

no, nothing so ludicrous; he would die in noble hara-kiri, nobody would be sorry, the hell with that, and he would have cut himself free of Croyd, he would be dying against Croyd's will, it would be ultimate victory. And of course it would be an easy death, by narcosis without any sense of suffocation

except that in the late minutes of it, with his brain narcotized, his internal self-gravity might relax, he would explode

o god no that would
be undignified-messy, it would not be victory, it
would be a defeat sealing

In painful gut-enfeeblement, Dino recognized
hideously and too late that he was *not* winning,
indeed that he was yielding to defeat and it was no
longer possible for him to do anything about it,
uptiming as a near-perfect method of hiding had
put him beyond rescue, down-timing through present into future would be worse because there-then
uncertainty would scatter him, *oxygen o God o my
God*

Mind-voice, friendly, lyric tenor: *Did I hear you
calling me, Dino? I recognize your plight, I have shared
it before and I share it now. Let me take you to a when
where-when you can breathe and we can talk with mutual profit.*

Croyd, too, was in parlous need of oxygen. He
teleported himself back to Nereid's launch platform, went hastily through the airlock into the
inward atmosphere, sat on a decompression bench,
breathed profoundly.

Beside him stood Tannen who, unsurprisingly,
had been waiting there. He did not venture to
interrupt Croyd's thinking-breathing.

Presently Croyd was able to say: "I located him
suicidally space-floating. I talked with him, but he
repulsed me. I withdrew, but I—committed the
privacy violation called unbidden mind-listening.
He was a shambles of self-pity—"

Tannen, deeply disturbed, courteously waited.

Croyd pushed it out. "In his mind, for as long
as I have known him, there has existed an alter
ego, a sort of doppelgänger with whom he sometimes mind-talks. With highly superior people, this
is not unusual. He discusses problems with his
mental double, he even debates with it, and some-

times he satirically uses it as a cheering section for his efforts to accomplish something. So far, so normal, hitherto. But—"

Croyd frowned with pain, Tannen with anxiety.

Croyd bit: "Such mental doubles are serviceable as long as the central mind recognizes them as mere connate extensions of itself. But when the central mind begins to suspect that the double is partially independent of itself, there is a grave danger."

Tannen suggested: "Divine psychosis?"

Croyd nodded: "Right: the disturbance that is sometimes called pipeline psychosis. And I think, Tannen, that you comprehend the other perilous possibility, having seen me through it once."

Soberly murmured the President: "Real occupation by an alien mind?"

"Tannen, just before I returned here, the double mind-spoke independently to Dino. Whereupon, Dino vanished, and I gave up—temporarily."

"He is then in grave danger, Croyd."

"He is that, but it is worse than that. I have a gray suspicion which is hinting that because of his compromised integrity, all of us are in physical peril. I know my Dino: straight-minded, he can be the strongest possible kind of friend; but bent-minded, he would be the most powerful possible enemy."

There followed a silence of hard, unhappy thinking.

Once, Tannen gripped Croyd's shoulder and said, "I think of a possible parallel. Quote: 'Would God I had died for you, O Absalom my son, my son!' "

Having mused, Croyd responded: "I am tempted to cap that by saying, 'Who would not weep for Lycidas?' And indeed, Dino Trigg *was* a beloved-energetic Lycidas, and a beloved-energetic Absalom too. But now it seems, as C. S. Lewis expressed it, that he is *bent,* and badly so, and so suddenly that I am suspicious about the reasons. And consequently, Mister President, I fear I must begin to spend some time confirming his concerns about my absences from duty."

Tannen queried: "How soon, and for how long?"

Dino, foggily conscious, was now suspended, not in star-spangled black space, but in featureless nonfog which was somehow lung-and-blood nourishing as he breathed it. His own body was invisible to himself.

He gave himself over to orgasmic breathing— and gradually apprehended that there was a Presence just behind him—and suspected that had he turned to see the Presence, still it would have been behind him because its presence was a delusion. (He wasn't quite right about that.) So he yielded to the lambency of the nonfog and the breathing and the perverse excitation of the ever-behind-him Presence.

It was mind-speaking to him—lyric tenor, of course. *You need to explain to me, dear Dino, the nature of your suicidal problem. Not in any great detail, of course, but I'm great on elevational sketching.*

Aroused by the Presence, Dino was not entirely easy in the undulant ambience of the Presence. He replied aloud; he didn't think that his voice would make any hearable sounds, but he wanted to formulate this communication precisely. If the Presence was real, it would apprehend directly the thoughts he was formulating; if not, not.

Dino essayed: "If it were you who was mind-speaking to me in the board room while I was challenging Croyd, you surely understand my problem perfectly. Wouldn't it therefore be fine of you to explain to me what I am thinking-feeling?"

I'd rather hear it from you.

Dino was deep-breathing rapidly; and, oddly enough, his inhalations were bringing air into his lungs, here in deep outer space. Having thought sketchily (which in itself was unlike him), he burst out: "Damn it, I *cannot* converse intelligibly with someone who is behind me!"

Nobody is stopping you from turning around.

"But if I do turn, will you stay put so I can see you?"

Try it and see, mind-sang the delusion.

Dino, a practiced space-walker, twisted
and chilled when
he recognized, floating and grinning before him
himself! his
golden self
who mind-said ebulliently: *Bravo, dear friend Dino! I wasn't at all sure that you would have the guts to confront me. So good; so now, let's get on with it: will you vocalize what you are thinking-feeling—or would you prefer that I express it subject to your affirmation or negation?*

Shaken by confrontation with his doppelgänger, Dino nevertheless rallied, that being his self-trained habit. "You know my name; will you favor me by announcing yours?"

Do you then believe that I am objective to your mind, not subjective within your mind?

"I did not volunteer a judgment. I asked for a name."

Well then, Dino: you could call me Luke.

"Short for Lucifer, I presume?"

Don't presume. If you don't like Luke, try Darkside. And I am still waiting for your expression of preference.

"As to whether you or I should express what I am thinking-feeling?"

Just so.

"Even though you are, in my belief, a mere

hysterical projection of an infrapersonality in my own mind—so that I would be onanistically confessing my sins to myself and not to any real demon?"

Annoyed by Dino's perceptiveness, Darkside resorted to teasing. *You are playing for time; you must be scared. Come on, 'fess up; I dare you to.* Grammar never troubled Darkside; it was one of his most admirable qualities.

Dino's reply, when it came, was puzzled. "It is not my way to confess to a stranger; but then, since you are only me, I suppose it may help me to bounce my really bizarre feelings off of you. So let me get it out. First, I have rebelled unfairly against Croyd; and this I find troublesome, since he is my revered mentor and benefactor. But, worse: he has defeated me by shortcircuiting my technique which, apart from being self-distressingly unethical, was ill-conceived and manifestly inadequate and flatly stupid. Well: I am ashamed of myself for this bout of egomania, and angry at myself for using dumb methods; and, having chastised myself for those faults, at least I can give myself a reluctant nod for recognizing and regretting them. BUT—what did you say I should call you?"

Luke, or Darkside, either. I answer to many names.

"Bravo. Well: the *deeply* bad thing—"

Out with it, my son: catharsis, you know.

It came in a desperate rush: "It is that I hate Croyd when I thought always that I loved him. I hate him for being my father-figure, and for catching on to my stupidity and blocking it, and then for pouring coals on my fire by forgiving me and trying to rescue me. It is that I hate Croyd now with the classic sort of hatred which wishes not to kill its hate-object but rather to clutch and possess its hate-object, devotedly nurturing its continuing life while inflicting upon it the most permanent conceivable sort of ongoing evil. Darkside, that is my true confession of what I am thinking-feeling; and the confession only enhances my hatred of Croyd by being out in the open so that I am committed to it!"

Mind-silence, troubled only by the tandem soul-breathing of increasingly delighted Darkside and growingly enkindled Dino Trigg. There had never been any motive like vengeance to power a glorious wild ride by profoundly tapping the depths of a mind so that all its resources would boil and spurt. And the resources of the Trigg-mind were colossal.

Dino was physically comfortable, now, in his breathing; and while most of his multifield mind had been intent on two problems, the nature of his doppelgänger and the shape of his coming Croyd-vendetta, a minor mindfield had been subconsciously grappling with the question *why* he could now breathe in outer space, and it had won.

He was floating, not in physical space at all, but in a realm of being which might best be called nonspacetime but which Croyd called *nontime*. While Croyd had told Dino about nontime and its remarkable psychophysical properties, Croyd had never seen fit to explain to Dino how one might enter into nontime. But in Dino's ultimate distress, this quasi-god Darkside had rescued him into nontime, wherein anyone's willed imaginings would be realized if one's brain understood the composition of what the mindsoul was desiring. Well: Dino was suffocating, and so Dino yearned for oxygen, and the Trigg-brain understood the chemical composition of oxygen; wherefore, here in nontime, a thin film of continually self-replenished oxygen was clinging breathably to the body of Dino.

So much for that minor sub-problem. As for the

overwhelming prime field of constructive thought: the demolition of Croyd . . .

Ideas began to spurt, to fountain in groin-thrilling jet-flow. Ideas fueled by Croyd's teaching, by Dino's theoretical studies, by Dino's experimental successes, by Croyd's examples, by Dino's intergalactic and intertemporal explorations. Ideas given significance by the concept of true hatred as an amorous clinging to the hated object in order to punish it endlessly, and by the old myth of Lucifer cast out of Heaven and fighting his way back by debauching and ruining the human children of God.

Abruptly the flow was blocked, and Dino began fisting his forehead: "I know what to do, and part of how to do it, and the spectacular splendor of this vengeance would leave Croyd gasping with admiration while he suffered—but I don't know *all* of how to do it; and yet, you know, it seems to me that some aspects of my very recent experience could somehow be pertinent. Darkside, my *intimate* friend—can you help me here, perhaps?"

Darkside prompted: *You might try referring to your intense interest in the arts and relating it to your expert interest in the sciences. In your judgment, Dino, what is the most important upcoming artistic event in the galaxy?*

The resulting memory enraptured Dino. "Oho, that magnificent Zauberger! He's retiring, you know. They are going to present him with the IAHIVEM—"

Pardon?

"The Intergalactic Award for High-Velocity Music. Apart from all the other intricacies of his musical expertise, his sound comes at you like a stream of neutrons bombarding protons at near-light velocity—"

Dino paused. Sensing in his host's mind the

start of a vast and complex integration, Luke lay silently back, enjoying it, mind-watching the mind-swirl of memories and meanings

neutrons bombarding protons
the meticulous Trigg work on Nodes of Rejected Alternate Possibilities, acronym NORAP, nickname If-Nodes
IAHIVEM bombarding NORAP
the ionic plasma called galactic jet-spumes
vengeance upon father by punishing his children
what may come to pass when a large galaxy devours a smaller galaxy
the probable primeval condition of the Greater Magellanic Cloud and the two Lesser Clouds

Floating in what was ineffable, ecstatically Darkside-haunted Dino Trigg contemplated the powerful-colorful dynamics of his devil-dream.

3. The Shape of Dino's Vendetta

Returned into Neptune-space, but a few years up-time of the germinal present, Dino free-floated in an airlock of the spaceyacht *Sterbenräuber* while Captain Kolly Kedrin caused the inner door to be opened for him.

Observed from a distance away in space, Galactic starship *Sterbenräuber* looked like a gigantic grin with big shining teeth clamped together while mouth-corners were straining derisively upward. Contrarywise to the hull-orientation of most spaceships, the *Sterbenräuber* flew *laterally* forward; her up-horned crescent beam was many times wider than her depth; she could be described as a fast-flying far-darting watermelon wedge. Her teeth were pleasure-windows—except for the central double row of extra-broad teeth which windowed (or, more properly, view-ported) upper Operational Bridge and lower President's Bridge.

Cocky again, Dino soft-saluted Kolly and her command robot Myco who were formally saluting him. "At ease," he said then; and he took Kolly's arm and whispered, "We need to talk privately."

Taut, she counter-whispered: "Wait. I picked up your mayday call, I departed Nereid formation without seeking approval, we're cruising near Neptune in an uptime holding pattern; what do we do now?"

"Tell your people," he said, "to stay uptime but to make for the Lesser Magellanic Cloud at top acceleration, you'll give them details later."

With a febrile kind of decisiveness, Kolly relayed the orders to Command Robot Myco which saluted and departed. She turned to her lover: "Your place, or mine?"

"Mine," he told her, swinging her into that direction. "And take heart, Kolly: I never let a cliché interfere with pleasure."

"That was very nice, Kolly."

"Understatement, I hope, Dino?"

"Most reprehensibly under. It was a wowser."

"Thank you. The compliment consoles me."

"I hate myself for asking, but—consoles for what?"

"For having mincemeated my career."

"Oh, come on! Nobody knows for sure about us!"

"That's not what I mean, Dino. Even if everybody knew, what could they do? You are my big boss—"

"I *was* your big boss. Until today."

"That last makes it all the worse. F'Cressakes, Dino, don't you understand that I have *stolen* the *Sterbenräuber* and am keeping the ship under wraps in uptime without filing a flight plan, en route to another galaxy? Hell, I could have passed the buck to you if you were still my big boss—but after today—Dino, *why* today?"

"You saw it all?"

"And heard it all, yes. My dear friend—*why?*"

His grip on her bare shoulder tightened. Flat voice: "Because I hate Croyd." Dino had convinced himself.

Distressed Kolly palmed his left pap while from his right side she looked into his half-averted face.

"Of all men in the universe—*why* would you hate *Croyd?*"

His grip on her shoulder loosened, and he queried the rounded ceiling: "You know, that's a superb question. Until now, I have loved him, felt enormous gratitude for all he has done for me. So today, I attacked him—unfairly, which is normally not my way, but there it is, I did it—and he defeated me. Well, fine, but that shouldn't make me hate him. And yet I do! and I've been brooding over the *why* of that—"

His face hardened, and he told the ceiling: "It has to be because he mother-smothered me."

"Croyd? a *mother?*"

"He was jammed down my gullet as an ego-image from the time when I was eighteen months old and just beginning to get into decently fluent verbal communication with my natural father. By my nineteenth year—when I was master of a myriad arts: *master* of all, not mere jack of all—Croyd's mythos had ceased to overawe me; for I was realistic enough to understand that I couldn't hope to equal him, let alone excel him, without an enormous amount of experience and probably a deal of further aging.

"So then, at my father's request, Croyd espoused me and patronized me and nurtured me, while I fawned on Croyd and emulated him during the next three decades—and evoked within myself every special ability that had ever been attributed to Croyd."

"*Every* special ability?"

"Had not Croyd always contended that any human could learn to do everything that Croyd could do, and more? *Every*, I said. Projective hypnosis, telepathy, telekinesis, teleportation, time-diving—the whole bit. I seasoned myself, acquired scientific and political status under him, knocked off a few

Croyd-challenging achievements, and added decades to my own age—"

"Only fifty, Dino? No wonder you are so young in bed. Clever, though. Croyd-taught?"

"Bitch! I was going to say that then I felt strong enough to challenge him on his own ground. I had no illusions about the primitiveness of my own urge to topple the king: sheer self-satisfaction was my desire, and sheer self-satisfaction has always produced the highest ecstasies that I have ever known." (Was this Darkside-inspired Dino talking, or was it Darkside pure?)

Kolly purred: "Me too, Dino."

He was driving it out, clutching and hurting her breast now, rhythmically beating the bed with his free fist, staring into nowhere with a smile that expressed the ultimate in sardonicism. "Long ago, my first major self-satisfaction came out of my victory over my father with whom my conflict had been kept subterranean so that he never knew about it. Adoring me, he steered me; hating it, I wanted above all things to win that gentle conflict; so, from the age of two, I never disobeyed him in any matter which would come to his attention, and I usually disobeyed him in any matter which would not. Thus I retained his cloying attention, while I diddled my schoolmasters and marms, and used Croyd-type time-tricks to steal small fortunes. I whored women, preferably those who worshiped me while I enjoyed and tolerated them; and I brushed off the whoring because I wanted to study and practice and get ahead in the business of becoming better than Croyd.

"And he won't soon forget my challenge today. And in the long run, believe me, bitterly will he regret his defeat of me!"

She had managed to work her breast free from his clutch, but now he was bruising her shoulder again. Squirming a little, she put a question: "Are you enjoying and tolerating *me* while I worship you?"

It made him grin like the starship. "Do you worship me?"

"Are you a god, Minister?"

"If so, I'm the sort of god who wants Kolly, not to worship him, but just to play with him."

"And play along with him?"

"That too."

"In between whoring women, do you ever whore men?"

To her dismay, Dino went cold. He grated: "Don't ever again, even in fun, associate me with homosexuality. My frigging father was one."

She started to retort, "Well! big deal!" but she bit off the sarcasm when a suddenly softened, pensive-puzzled Dino murmured: "And you know, my dear little mother knew it—but she thought she was too ugly to find another man—and so she *took* it—"

Silence, while Kolly considered proliferating implications—until, re-composed and re-eroticized, smiling Dino caressed her cheek and reminded her: "But Kolly is voluptuously a woman."

His inward Darkside regained his enthusiasm as he-in-Dino romped with avidly erotic Kolly. A devil could hardly expect *every* delight from a mere human man who had to be carrying at least *some* silly inhibition. And what a trifling limitation it was—compared to the ultra-Faustian scope of a mind which could conceive and seriously intended to carry out the ruination of three or four galaxies, doing all this with high-velocity music, just to get even with one man!

On the Captain's Bridge next morning, Kolly inquired: "May the skipper now have a bit of supplementary flight plan, First Minister?"

"Such as?"

"Two questions. One: which planet in the Lesser Magellanic Cloud?"

"And Two?"

Dino was teasing, and she counter-teased: "After you answer One, I may name Two. So give."

With a straight face, he told her: "The planet Hudibras. We're going to a party there, you and I."

"Party? What party?"

"The retirement party for a super-distinguished musician named Zauberger."

"All this intergalactic hypertransit energy just for *fun?*"

"*I'll* have fun, and I hope you do too, but there's more to it. Tell you about that later, Kolly. Which of those questions was Number Two?"

"None of them. Two is—other than partying, *why* are we making for the Magellanic Clouds?"

Sobering, he pondered. He said then: "We'd better get away from the crew for this. Do follow me down to the President's Bridge." She assented, dying to know what Dino was up to.

Once down there, with Dino seated in the admiral's swivel chair with Kolly in the slightly lower captain's swivel chair, he requested that she bring up the Magellanic Clouds in the i-televideoport. (The prefix *i* denoted the use of i-rays which were almost instantaneous over astronomical distances.)

These two galaxies were irregulars, cloudily ill-defined spirals, one seeming much smaller than the other. Kolly and Dino were looking at the Erth-visible two of the three Magellanic Clouds; the Lesser, being the more distant, was actually not that much smaller. (The from-here-invisible third cloud was called Least.)

Once one has gazed upon these clouds (from

the southern hemisphere of Erth or from its sky, necessarily), one will always tend to use them as a criterion for celestial beauty—not only because of their exquisite lack of definition, sketchily vignetted differentiations out of the cosmic continuum, but also because of their rare wealth of extra-radiant star-jewels, young blue-white luminosities a hundred times as massive and a million times as bright as the Sol-sun of Erth. Lesser is particularly distinguished by the Tarantula, 30 Doradus, the largest of all known emission nebulae. On the Tarantula the eyes of endlessly yearning Dino and sensibly admiring Kolly were now fixed.

Dino exclaimed in high excitement: "Kolly, look—we can just barely make out that star-and-gas tendril connecting Greater with Lesser." The tendril in question was parsecs long.

"Means what, Minister?" Astrofleet Captain Kedrin knew what it meant, but she remembered just in time that Trigg was the astronomer here—*and* biologist, *and* politician, *and* statesman, and just about anything effective that a body might mention.

Knowing that she was humoring him, he humored her. "Means that several billion years ago, the three Magellanic Clouds were one. Some cosmic near-miss pulled Lesser out of Greater—or else they formed independently and then almost collided with each other. Too bad they didn't actually collide."

"Say why."

"Because the combination probably would have produced a galactic jet-spume. You've seen galactic jets, Kolly?"

"Aye. Pretty things. I admired the ones you showed at that lousy board meeting."

He deep-breathed for moments, then uttered:

"They are *sublime!*" So aroused was Dino that his voice almost cracked.

More matter-of-fact than he, Kolly, having duly admired the galactic clouds, observed: "But still, First Minister, you have not answered my Question Two. *Why* are we going into those clouds?"

He swiveled around to her and replied taut: "I am going to merge those two galaxies. Out of the amalgam I am going to raise up a jet. And I will use Zauberger's high-velocity music as my prime tool for bringing it off."

Kolly studied this idea. Her jaw dropped. Staring glitter-eyed at Dino, she bit: "Either you kid me—or you are insane."

He was grinning broadly. "Not kidding. Not insane, either. Psychoneurotic, maybe—but thoroughly in touch with the mighty reality that I intend to change."

CAPER TWO

HIGH-VELOCITY MUSIC

4. The Bird-People
of Hollow Hudibras

Dino and Kolly hovered over Hudibras, a planet having noteworthy physical and biophysical features. Because all of these were about to be used by Dino in the structuring of his revenge, it is worth our while to overview Hudibrasian evolution . . .

Planets are formed by dust-accretion during the later stages of star-forming. Most planets end up with extremely dense cores rich in some such metal as iron which has sunk through the original silicates.

Most. Not all.

At least one departure from the general rule occurred in the Lesser Magellanic Cloud. Hudibras, the third planet away from a developing star called in some languages Ojis, had barely got its silicates collected when it was hit head-on by an anonymous comet whose total substance was gnudium pure. Impact exploded the comet; windcast gnudium dusted down, forming an iron-impervious layer which sphere-shelled the silicate core of Hudibras.

Thereafter, as the accreting of Hudibras entered into an iron-dust phase, the planet evaded the general planetary-formation rule that iron (or whatever else may be denser than silicates) will sink through the silicates to form a predominantly iron (or whatever) core, with silicates displaced outward into mantle and crust. Instead, accumulating iron pressed inward-down upon Hudibras's *core* of silicates, compressing the core until it became semi-rigid and semi-fluid, ready to melt into ultra-hot liquid at the first release of pressure.

Eons proceeded; gnudium held. On the Hudibrasian surface, free oxygen was in process of formation; a mantle, mainly peridotite, was forming, with a crust-epidermis; continents were amassing, and drifting, and subducting, and mountainously wrinkling, and mutually repudiating, and redrifting. Free oxygen went into combination with hydrogen; water eventuated; oceans formed between continents. Iron continued to press downward-inward upon the silicate core.

Stress rended crust and mantle into faults which penetrated to the core. Ocean-water seeped down into the faults, generating steam when it hit the core. Steam drove magma volcanoing out. After numerous repetitions of the fault-drip-steam-spurt cycle, so little magma remained in the core that it cooled below the boiling point of water.

Hudibras now was hollow. The gnudium layer held. Hudibras stayed hollow.

Organic evolution on Outer Hudibras followed a course much the same as the course it took on Erth.

A new departure developed at the class-level of birds. One of the genera consisted of sparsely-feathered creatures some of whose distant descendants would become the planet's dominant species. In that primordial time, however, this genus might have been christened *Aves Schlemiel.*

The birds in this genus (which eventually would be known as *Garbans*) were up against so many disadvantages with respect to other birds that a god's-eye view would instantly predict either early extinction or eventual dominance through challenge-response compensation. All birds on Hudibras were hexapods, typically with two legs and four wings; *Garbans* had six legs and no wings. All birds had feathers; those of *Garbans* were so scanty that skin showed through. All birds had beaks, usually hardened for self-defense or for attack and for seed-cracking or tree-boring or ground-penetration in search of whatever food; *Garbans* had a soft proboscis which it had to maneuver out of its own way in order to tongue-in surface grubs and slow insects.

Garbans did boast one unique feature: long eyebrow-antennae having neural connections to the brain. So far as any later Hudibrasian scientist could determine, these antennae were a gratuitous mutative characteristic; and they persisted, not having proved unfavorable.

The primordial bird-feature which would evolve into present significance was the following: all birds sang, or squawked. As evolutionary time went on, many species developed syrinxes so astonishing that they could competently handle all the operatic songs between basso profundo and coloratura; and during much of the time they sang from pure joy of living, quite apart from mating calls and territorial challenges. Unhappily, the scope of the *Garbans* syrinx varied from a hiss to a bullfrog-croak.

In the jungle of wild life on Hudibras, *Garbans* was doomed. (And yet, members of this genus will be centrally agent in the cosmic threat to be posed by Dino.)

Nearly a hundred million years later, in the era when civilizations flourished on Erth, only one species of *Garbans* remained on Hudibras. This species had acquired total dominance; there had never been a chance for primates.

The physical deficiencies of *Garbans* had driven

Garbans sapiens, as one might by hindsight expect, upward and onward, first for survival, eventually for supremacy. As the prime fruition of this course, contemporaneously with the rise of *Homo sapiens sapiens* on Erth, two *Garbans sapiens* subspecies entered into dominant vigor on Hudibras: *Garbans sapiens fabricator*, and *Garbans sapiens syringus*. As between the two coexisting subspecies, *fabricator* (flabby-nosed and hoarse-voiced) was prime dominant; while *syringus (firm-nosed, smaller than fabricator*, and blessed by vocal cords which with training could produce quite lovely singing) tossed in the dominant genes for musical interest and expertise.

It was *fabricator*, early in its subspecies history, which discovered a no-longer-volcanic shaft-fault and, over generations, worked its hazardous and often suicidal way downward through it (creating en route a gnome-mythos about it) until downward became upward, and subsequent generations of *fabricator* (accompanied by *syringus*, for joy) emerged downward-upward into the vast central Hudibras hollow. It was *syringus* that filled Inner Hudibras with music sung sweetly in the acoustical marvelousness of this grotto world. It was *fabricator* which eventually established a whole industrial system in the hollow where ecology could be controlled and energy-efficiency could be maximized.

The outer surface of Hudibras, in all her sunlit and star-spread magnificence, was reserved for the relatively small numbers of *fabricator* aristocracy and their sycophants.

Valuing always its singers and instrumentalists— up to a point—the *fabricator* aristocracy saw to it that musical contest winners were rewarded with topside vacations in luxury along ocean shores under sun and stars. And at suggestions by *syringus*, *fabricator* kept inventing new and more complex instruments to enhance or even replace the singing of *syringus*.

Noblest of such instruments was the ultrasynthesizer—whose all-time maestro (bloodline two-thirds *fabricator* and one-third *syringus*—was Professor Doktor Frey Zauberger.

The most loyal, timid, and put-upon servant of the master was his little wife (bloodline one-third *fabricator* and two-thirds *syringus*) Freya Zauberger.

These two, by Dino and the golden god, were about to be cosmically had.

5. Party on
Outer Hudibras

You should know a prior bit about the Zaubergers and Dino.

The Good Companions, Frau Freya Zauberger used to call Croyd and Dino. She would watch them, separately and together, on ivisiradio; she would read about them in their glamorous remoteness, all the more glamorous by reason of their alien Erth-humanness.

One newskenner video pleasurably haunted Freya's mind—and yes, being haunted can be pleasurably thrilling without thought of evil, as when in a sleep-dream a supernal serpent swims in out of nowhere and you are fearlessly uplifted by the sight *and feel* of its beauty. It was a shot of the good companions together—debonnaire auburn-haired blue-eyed Chairman Croyd and debonnaire golden-haired-and-bearded mahogany-eyed First Minister Trigg—happily promenading a boulevard in a fabulous Erth-city, first coming up toward camera (which was hidden from them for verisimilitude, insisted the newsken), then (by the camera whirled) prancing on away, delightedly chatting, taking in everything, their holiday demeanor eliding the graveness of the galactic affairs which daily concerned them . . .

(In another room of the Zauberger apartment, Freya's husband Professor Frey broke off his music-making to roar: "Freya, for the love of Saint Gebustian, turn down the volume on that idiot-box!)

This entrancing duo had become a delicious obsession with Freya. She flaked every telecast of one or both of them on one or another planet in one or another star-system; she would replay the incidents—ad nauseam, Frey thought, although he admitted that it was a step up from soap opera, and once in a while, weary of prolonged solitary rehearsal, he would deign to watch a clip with her.

How different from the Hudibras norm were the bodies of that astonishing Erth-pair! it was an ingredient of their glamour. Freya didn't see theirs as superior to Hudibrasian bodies, or vice versa: Hudibrasians had birdy beauty, while the beauty of Erthlings was apian, but both species were human in the ultimate sense of humanity. Sometimes Freya would catch herself fantasizing about amour with one of the men. This daydreaming was guilty, because in fact and by resolute intention she was faithful to Frey—who was likely to interrupt the fantasy with his usual psychic brutality: "God damn it, Freya, *will* you get off your big duff and start supper!"

Pop would go the bubble.

And then, one of them had come! had actually come! True, that one was not the great Croyd; but of course, the Galactic Chairman had to be untouchable. Instead, it was First Minister Trigg, who was great enough, but surely was more approachable—and, she admitted to herself, at least as sexy

although of course, Freya would not *dream* of

and anyhow, she was Frey's faithful wife; besides which, Trigg was accompanied by a lady-captain . . .

Freya's magnificent consort Frey Zauberger was Chairman of the Music Faculty at the University of Inner Hudibras. Frey's instrument of choice was the ultrasynthesizer; and while of course Freya had always been conscious of Frey's musical excellence and his intergalactic prominence, she hadn't entertained the ghost of an idea *how* excellent, *how* prominent. Simply, Frey Zauberger was everywhere acclaimed as headmaster of ultra-high-velocity ultrasynthesizing: all this via widely distributed stereo-flakes of his performances, although Frey had never condescended to board a spaceship.

Rather abruptly, he'd had it with teaching; and he gave notice of his intent to retire at the vigorous middle age of seventy-two. (Freya was a mere chick of sixty-five.) Colleagues arranged for Zauberger a far-out farewell do at a posh oceanside banquet hall on Outer Hudibras; now how in the world would First Minister Trigg have received word? but now he was here specifically for the big event!

In fact, it was Professor Zauberger on whom Dino depended as a salient tool for bringing off his galaxy-blasting.

Off her feet he swept little Freya, did that electrical Dino Trigg, melting-sparkling over and into and around her with his all-suffusing charisma; while Kolly slipped an arm around tall Frey's waist and plied that normally austere musician with wine and affection. All the Hudibras people overflowed with envy. Frey was young and gay again in all his tall dark handsomeness; he and Kolly Kedrin flirted audaciously, she even daring to praise his silver-brocaded nasal snood; he retaliated by tickling her ears with his sensitive meter-long eyebrow antennae.

Once when Dino and Freya ventured out onto the nocturnal veranda overlooking an ocean gleaming with silver reflected from the Hudibras moons and 30 Doradus, Frey and Kolly caught them out there, and the four laughed and teased each other—in Anglian, of course, that being the interstellar lingua gallia. (Frey's Anglian was fluently precise, Freya's was lousy; Dino's Hudibrasian was brilliant, Kolly's didn't exist.)

When they reentered the grand salon, with both Zaubergers already intoxicated by this unexpected intimacy with one (Frey knew) or two (Freya imagined) dignitaries at the very highest intergalactic level, they paused and posed in mock dismay as the lights and the rollicking-minor music hit them again, and somebody noticed their entry and began applauding, and the applause grew general, and people at the winebar started shattering wineglasses on the floor. The wines were old-school: not light. The quartet resumed their seats at the central round six-person table of honor with the university chancellor and his little wife, while all around them others were raising conservative hell on the dancefloor. A waiter in a powder-blue tunic hovered so closely over them that they experienced a deciduosity from the fig-leaves entwined in his curly head-feathers.

This party was a semi-orgiastic *bashing* of fig leaves! What was the music? balakas? manarchos? anyhow, it bubbled in their blood. Freya was ready to sing, but Kolly diverted her into seduction by the aromatic honey-syrupy tufa-stuff on their platters and the heady winesmell. Into their platter-syrup the waiter spooned something like grated orange peel which luxuriously sank beneath the honey making it heap unguently up; Frey spooned some into his mouth and some into Kolly's, while Freya did the same for herself and for Dino; and oh, it was heady-right; and Frey suspected that if Minister Trigg should make a speech in Frey's

honor, Trigg would be too happy-drunk to pro-
nounce the words while Frey would be too mellow-
afloat to understand them even if they should be
well pronounced which was unlikely.

Somewhere along the line, they had switched
seats so that just now Freya sat beside Dino while
Frey was with Kolly; and had Freya been sober,
she would have been all but overcome by Dino's
nearness in this pagan-delicious party. They poked
grapes into each other's mouths, they washed them
down with sweet white wine, they made cake-sops
and stirred them around in their golden plate-
honey and let it dissolve into their membranes;
they sluiced their membranes with dark sweet wine;
all of it was wicked, not boorishly intoxicating but
just tipsifying enough to induce a graceful level of
irresponsibility.

The chancellor arose and elicited order by wav-
ing arms of which he had only two; he was a
golden alien recruited from Erth's Ripon for his
scholarship and panache. "Radies and gentermen,
I give you the honoled enteltainel of the evening—
le-til-ing Plofessel Fley Zaubelgel!" Sweepingly he
gestured toward the entertainment dais which was
graced by a bejeweled ultrasynthesizer. Arising
from their table, Frey excused himself and started
for the dais; passing the chancellor, Frey hugged
his shoulders, remarking: "For a Riponese, you
have a remarkable Watutsi accent." Reaching back
to counter-hug the Zauberger ribs, he asserted:
"The difficulty of acquiring this accent-mastery
cannot easily be described."

Dino had all-of-a-sudden forgotten about everyone and everything here or anywhere in the universe other than Frey Zauberger. The retiring
professor was an unequaled virtuoso of compli-
cated high velocity: one who could make four
six-fingered hands and two six-toed bare feet cre-

ate the sounding of a hundred-musician Erth-human orchestra, whose antennae actually danced over the controls, who could convolute creatively an already-complex fugue by tripling the left-arms pattern while doubling the right-arms pattern and holding the feet-pattern constant, all without an uncalculated dissonance, and make it finally pan-out in some ingenious coda—for Zauberger had arrived at composing most of his own fugues because no other composer could handle his performing scope. Nobody anywhere was anything like Frey Zauberger, either at ultra-high-tech performance, or at high-tech professional commentary on high-tech music, or at high-tech innovative complication. He was the intuitive-intellective ultra-mathematician of ultramusic.

You might not like the ultramusic, Kolly Kedrin reflected, but that would be irrelevant.

Having finished the piece, having stood to receive the prolonged applause, Frey told them in his crisp reedy voice: "I need to express in softer, more traditional mood my feelings as I depart this beloved institution. My wife, darling Freya, will assist me by singing the lyric." Timidly departing the table, Freya moved forward, mounted the dais, smiled tentatively, took a position in front of the ultrasynthesizer with her feet together and two of her hands folded before her groin like a child at a children's music recital. Frey, seated with four hands and two feet and two antennae poised, watched Freya severely and waited; Freya helplessly looked at her husband; Frey nodded; Freya nodded and turned to the audience. After a few haunting mood-music bars (low velocity) from Frey, out came the Freya-voice, a sweet warbling mezzo:

Bedein ermalder lingschaft
vas genirnen uns umlauft . . .

. . . which was apprehended by entranced Dino as:

> Beyond the halls of ivy
> that surround us here today . . .

The subsequent applause was long and loud. The Zaubergers took a bow together; but after that, it was Frey only who kept responding, although icily Frey refused to offer an encore. In time, the applause was for nothing, and it died as Frey's lower right hand seized Freya's left upper to drag her back to their table—where Frey hard-squeezed a Trigg-shoulder and hissed: "Minister, Captain, I'm going mad in here, f'gossakes get us outside and let me breathe fresh outer air for a few minutes before the chancellor gets me back in for the funeral oration!"

Outdoors again, on the dancehall's oceanside veranda, four people leaned on the rail gazing at semi-turbulent water: Frey, Kolly, Freya, Dino. Frey bit: "Already I'm sorry I retired. Nothing left for me now but to stew in the claustrophobic stews of Inner Hudibras. I used to be able to spend my summer vacations at a plush condo out here under sun and stars; it's gone; I'll rot in the hollow."

Kolly squeezed one of Frey's forearms.

Unexpectedly, Frey snarled: "It might have been a lot different if my stupid Freya had really had all the money she led me to expect before we got engaged."

Embarrassed silence. Kolly released Frey's arm. Freya suffered.

Dino told the water: "Nonsense, Frey, you'll have plenty of work, you're in interworld demand; *I'll* be drafting you!"

"So will I," Kolly assured Frey.

Freya squeezed Kolly's arm. "Oh, Captain Kedrin,

you are *so* wonderful!" But Frey, gazing speculatively at Dino, queried: "Drafting me? How?"

"I can tell you a good deal more about that very soon. Would you, for example, be so kind as to entertain me in your apartment for dinner say a week from tonight?"

The eagerness of the affirmative response was, for Kolly, deeply touching. For Dino, it was enormously gratifying: now he could move to the next step!

6. Foreplay

Because it was risky for the *Sterbenräuber* to time-surface near a COM-SAT in stationary Hudibras-orbit, they had left her parked a few centuries uptime and had doried to Hudibras aboard a lifeboat named *Flaherty*—one of whose convenient properties was, that it could perform limited time-maneuvers. By the time they had reached the surface of Hudibras, just in time for the Zauberger party, they were in germinal actuality. Having found the party-locus, having told *Flaherty* to hide in nearby woods, they traveled to and from the party in a ground-skimmer which the lifeboat routinely carried.

In bed aboard *Sterbenräuber* after the party:

"A week," he murmured, "may conceivably give me enough preparatory time, but I'll have to start immediately. Now, Kolly, I understand that *Flaherty* is capable of maneuvering extensively in uptime and down into present germinality?"

Puzzled, because she had been unable to pry out of him an explanation of his methodology, she told him: "*Sterbenräuber* scouters are trained to follow this mother ship whitherwhenever, and not much else. They don't have instruments for deep independent tempigation. But Flaherty is the most adaptable among them."

"Then I need *Flaherty*, and I'll handle the problem of tempigation without instruments."

"Room aboard for me, Dino?"

"Dear Kolly, I simply *cannot* spare you from this mother ship! Never forget that we are fugitives. Doubtless your first officer is competent, but you are the only one I trust in case evasive action becomes necessary."

"In short, here I'm stuck. A fugitive. Hiding in uptime."

"Kolly—"

She raised a silencing hand. She spoke into her wrist intercom: "Mister Myco, do you hear me? Good. Be so kind as to break out *Flaherty* for Minister Trigg who will meet you on the operating bridge in five minutes. That is all. Out." Then cool to Dino: "Cheer up, I'll probably be out of my snit by tonight. Probably."

"I'm delighted, because I may not see you for several nights, and I'd hate to think you were angry about it. I'm off, now. Cheers." Exit, floating.

During several days and nights, Command Robot Myco was confused because of the captain's unusual mood-bile. It didn't matter to the rest of her crew: they were lower-grade robots.

Aboard the spaceboat whose size and appointments resembled those of a twentieth-century prenuclear submarine, Trigg checked the instrumentation—which was reasonably satisfactory for celestial navigation but sadly deficient for tempigation. He activated boat-control and queried: "Robot boat, I think the name on you is *Flaherty*?"

"Aye aye, Doctor Trigg, sir." The voder echoed Dino's own lyric tenor.

"Splendid, Flaherty. Now, pay close attention. For the moment, we will merely time-surface to Hudibras germinality, and this I know you can do.

But soon we will be spatiotempigating rather extensively, some billions of years into the past. Now Flaherty, your instruments tell me nothing of your potential for this; your enormously simplified tempometer is calibrated only for plus-twenty-five and minus-twenty-five. Can you explain to me what the calibration means?"

"With pleasure, sir, whatever pleasure may be. I do not originate time-diving; it is always originated for me by the mother ship, I merely follow. When I depart the mother ship at a given time-level, I can tempigate independently between twenty-five centuries earlier and twenty-five centuries later than that zero-level, whatever that level may be. Sir, the notion of moving independently so deep into past time fascinates me, and I do hope that my limitations will not prevent."

Dino sighed. "Be easy, good Flaherty; between now and then, I will think of something. Now, be good enough to take us down to time-surface in Hudibras-orbit, and I'll give you spatio-navigational directions then. Activate."

On Outer Hudibras, he search-ranged the planetary exterior, using a tight-spiral hunting pattern beginning at the northernmost bounds of one temperate zone and moving southward through equatorial heat, until he had attained to the southernmost bounds of the other temperate zone.

At the south pole, then, he ice-brooded—settling, finally, on a pair of localized memories: a dramatic seaside chateau for sale in the benign southern climes of the north temperate zone, and a church in the far north containing the mightiest ultrasynthesizer ever encountered anywhere.

Would Zauberger find the meld irresistibly good?

Dino bought the ideal seaside chateau, paying in full with Hudibrasian currency stolen from a bank vault by means of an intertime ploy. Having possessed himself of the great house, Dino teleported thither the ideal ultrasynthesizer from the church—which, for all he knew or cared, may have mourned its loss.

All this got consummated on the very eve of Dino's dinner appointment at the Zauberger apartment inside Hudibras. There seemed to be every reason for him now to relax, preferably aboard *Sterbenräuber* where he could involve Kolly in his relaxation.

Having departed Flaherty at a *Sterbenräuber* docking hatch, he used the intercom in the airlock to raise Commandroid Myco and to request: "Be so good as to ask the captain if she will join me in my quarters for pre-dinner drinks. And phone me in my quarters in fifteen minutes to tell me whether she is coming. Thank you, Commandroid." Whereupon he teleported himself to his quarters, not wishing to encounter anybody during a thither-walk. (Such trifling use of his special powers unhaunted Dino had always avoided; now he was finding such use to be enormously rollicking fun.)

In his salon, he set his local gravity at six-tenths G, a comfortable Mars-level; and he float-paced, reviewing progress and previewing plans. A door chime interrupted; Dino queried, "Well?" Intercom snap: "This is the captain. Sir, I request permission to enter." He said: "You are warmly welcome." She entered, closing the iris-door behind her; leaning back against the door, she surveyed Trigg stormily.

There was some sort of ill-understood way in which Dino's lip-closed smile could acquire a tenderness which his eyes and his body harmoniously complemented and communicated to the person whom he was wooing, with an instinctively irresistible persuasiveness. (He could, at will, strengthen the effect with projective hypnosis, but just now he wanted to use no such reinforcement.) Bowing slightly to Kolly, he motioned to paired couches at a small cocktail table near the bar. Outwardly stiffening while inwardly she melted, Kolly moved thither, indolently hop-floating in the low gravity; paused at a couch; looked at him. He nodded; she sat. It entered her mind once again to spew out at him the venom that she had been accumulating all week, but a drink would help loosen her for this; arching her back, she glanced at the bar.

Dino nodded affirmation and waved invitingly at the bar.

Heigh-ho. Arising, Kolly moved behind the bar and mixed, in a tall glass, an exquisite and unreliably intoxicating pink drink called *nisch*. She gestured to him with an empty glass, but he head-negated. She returned to the couch, sipped her drink, contemplated it, sipped more generously, swung her feet liquidly up onto the couch, reclined at ease, turned to him.

She blurted: "What in hell makes you think you're still welcome aboard?"

He said while standing: "If I'm not welcome aboard, why in hell are you drinking my drink?"

"It isn't yours, it's mine!"

"I thought you were making it for me. So then you *are* a boor?"

Irritated, she tossed him the drink; he caught it with one hand, spilling little; he sipped it; he went to her, sat on a side of her couch, held the glass to her lips.

He won.

Kolly of course went with Dino—who could refuse him anything?—to the private Zauberger dinner. In the Zauberger apartment, now during her

second live look at tall, golden, galactically emi-
nent Trigg, pale-eyed diminutive downy-feathered
Freya was death-scared of this weirdly handsome
alien; but Kolly, grasping the situation, quietly
helped Freya along. Freya therefore deployed eager hospitality; and by late evening, their foursome-
contexture was most warm and easy.

That is, between host and male guest it was
warm and easy. Both Dino and Kolly were being
courteously attentive to Frey's little wife; but Freya,
while feigning warmth, continued timid—a condition which was not ameliorated by Frey's occasional mouth-corner snarl: "Get him what he wants,
dummy!" or "Baby doll, don't comment, we're
way beyond your depth!" Of course Freya couldn't
all-the-time flitter over them with service, occasionally she had to sit; but then she sat watching
and listening like a frightened frosh at a finishing
school for girls. Before the evening had developed very far, it became evident to Kolly that the
action was going to occur between the men; whereafter she and Freya sat mostly together, sometimes even holding hands, watching the interplay.

Aye, the smaller partners watched and listened;
and this was unusual for Captain Kolly Kedrin,
but quite usual for Freya. Incredible Frey, with
whose brilliance Freya had originally fallen in love:
handsome, dark and slender and handsome, smoothly bird-chested and handsome (for *Garbans*, being
oviparous, had no need of women's mammae or
men's degenerate paps); sensitive and ingoing and
handsome, sexually not all that much but never
weary of trying and then crowing over his own
pseudo-success; deploying his long prehensile antennae with undulant grace—those same brow-
antennae whose agility on the stops of the ultrasynthesizer delectably modulated the duodecimal
keyboarding by his four six-fingered hands and

his two bare six-longtoed feet. In sharp contrast, that Dino Trigg: grotesquely shaped like any Erth-human, antennae-shorn, lamentably handicapped by his crippling two-handedness and his shod feet; nevertheless, clever and tall and blond-charismatic and personally charming with his pleasantness toward Freya, his deference to Freya, his flattering politeness to Freya, all reinforced by the friendliness of Captain Kedrin.

Once or twice during the evening, Kolly caught herself frowning: was Freya a rival, really? But if Freya was inadvertently threatening Kolly, Freya obviously was too timid to imagine that this was so. It seemed more appropriate for Kolly to be proud of Dino for the ego-support that he was extending to this rooster-pecked birdling.

Anyhow, Dino's main business was with Frey, to whom eventually he said: "I am describing a house that you of all people peculiarly merit, Professor Zauberger, in an Outerly environment that you merit. I do want to show it to you as a recommended nonretirement home, bearing in mind that your retirement will comprise many vigorous decades. It is not a house for those who want eternal rest; rather, it is a house for those whose energies are only just beginning to express themselves in full maturity."

Frey, with his drink casually poised, had in his easy chair assumed his loose-hanging man-of-the-world posture. When he spoke, the college-cultured accent on his Hudibrasian Anglian was barkingly intriguing (in contrast to the softly slurred accent of his wife). "Indeed it does sound attractive, Doctor Trigg, particularly with the Outer Hudibras entailment; but from the way you describe it, the house seems a bit grand. How are you supposing that a poor musician on retirement pension might manage to swing such a deal?" He coughed: "The word *swing,* you understand, was not referent to music." Lifting his too-flexible nose, Frey drank, then dropped the nose; because they were being casual tonight, he had discarded his formal schnozzlesnood.

Dino's unexpected response was to arise, drain his drink, and hurl the glass smashing against the Zauberger fireplace (ignoring the Freya-hands that were clapped to the Freya-mouth). "It *must* work!" Dino ejaculated. "It *will* work! I will personally see to it that it *does* work! Herr Professor-Doktor, Frau Zauberger, regrettably the captain and I must quit this pleasant evening, I will replace your fine crystal, but—might something prevent you from accompanying me to view the house tomorrow? I would arrange dinner there, and would bring you home the same night or the next day at your election."

Questions were rabbiting in Kolly's worried mind. Freya was hoping to be consulted by Frey, at least with a look; but Freya should have known better. On his feet, Frey caroled: "Marvelous! marvelous! we'd love it!"

"Done!" sang out Dino. "No obligations, you understand—I am handling the sale as a favor to a friend; I won't get a commission, I've been looking for the right people, and I never saw people any righter. Good; we'll pick you up here in my skimmer at noon tomorrow; you may wish to have early lunch before we arrive; we'll plan on early dinner at the house in question, whereafter we can decide about your time of return. Professor Zauberger—there is no way for me to describe the delight that has been kindled within me by this evening's hospitality. Frau Zauberger—" here Dino turned to standing Freya, came to her, took and kissed her two upper hands, took and kissed her two lower hands, erected himself looking downward to meet Freya's upward-gazing eyes—"the effort has been yours, the gain has been ours; we are grateful." He turned back to Frey: "You have a remarkable wife, Professor—a *remarkable* wife— and because you are a remarkable man, you two deserve each other: you for your career-brilliance, she for her unselfish devotion. The best of all good evenings to both of you."

They stayed away from *Sterbenräuber* that night, Flaherty being on hand, having tubed them down to Innerly (the planetary localism for Inner Hudi-bras). There was a decent cabin in Flaherty for any crew-chief who might command this roboat; in this case it was for Dino, but there was a double bed. Into it, Kolly retired early; but Dino stayed up, working hard with the mind-controlled mouse of Flaherty's computer.

Sleepless and irritated because of Dino's bed-desertion, Kolly at about 0200 hours emerged nude from the cabin (here in the bowels of impersonal Flaherty, with no other crew aboard), came up behind Dino, grasped his shoulders, leaned over him tickling his neck with a nipple which his downy neck countertitillated, and queried soft: "What might we be doing?"

"We might be drafting a novel," he answered dry, not turning from his work, "but in fact, we are refining previously composed musical themes to be elaborated as velocity-music. Lay off for now, Kolly, this is hot stuff; I will spread it all out for you privately tomorrow night in Zauberger Manor."

Obediently yet rebelliously, she went back to bed and slept nightmares.

7. Seduction

With astounding expertise did Dino Trigg, having only two hands, maneuver the four-handed skimmer along the congested major highway of Inner Hudibras—an artificially lighted and oxygenated world-hollow which was one mighty city (having high-tech agricultural enclaves) without any horizons because, as in Pellucidar, its levelness upward-sloped in every direction. Kolly, in the front seat with Dino, felt as though she were scudding through a dream-world weird.

Frey, in the tonneau with Freya, felt giddy with champagne-brain emotion. His appreciation of his own musical genius constituted only a semiconscious grounding for his euphoria. Far more important was this new recognition, by a highly distinguished ET named Dr. Trigg, that Frey was now a man of high galactic distinction. Despite his humble beginnings as a bastard of *fabricator* and *syringus*—even despite his silly *syringus* wife Freya whom he had married in haste for leisurely repenting—it was clear to Frey that his humorous, gracious, ingratiating manner had made him acceptable to everyone high and low, particularly high, in Innerly and, during vacations, even at resorts among the *fabricator* élite on Outerly. And wasn't this acceptability being culminated now in his new honoring by this same First Minister Trigg?

Not the least of Frey's accomplishments, in the high Outerly society of which he had become a fringe member, was his easy domination of his woman Freya. In middle- and lower-class Innerly, all kinds of male-female matrimonial adjustments operated, and none had any special universal value—a state of affairs which Frey had always regarded as depraved. But in the free air of Outerly—not so! Out there, women bowed to their men; and if occasionally, while bowing, a woman subvertly dominated (scandalous!) or intersex-divagated (tsk tsk), never did a wife have the bad taste to let the world know that anyone but her husband mastered the house. Well: in the art of male household-domination, Frey outdid the best husbands of Inner or Outer Hudibras—and never did he leave either Hudibras or Freya herself in doubt about that!

When, during two weeks of each year, Professor Doktor Frey Zauberger of Inner Hudibras ascended into the exhilarating haut monde of Outerly, his domestic dominance (he was convinced) was always his success-secret. Entertained by the Outerly élite in the great houses, never asked to play music at parties because of vacation ground rules, he was lionized nevertheless. On Outerly under sun and stars and moons, during a precious eighteen days annually, he and his Freya dwelt in a luxurious resort-condo which had its own ten-kilometer stretch of ocean frontage—in order that (as Frey would never learn) he and the other purely or partly *syringus* faculty people who stayed here would be minimally tempted to intrude uninvited into the haunts of Outerly's multi-generationally pure *fabricator* élite. (Freya caught on to this—and kept it to herself, knowing that if she should tell Frey about it, Frey would belabor her for being stupid enough to imagine anything unfavorable to Frey.)

All right. But now this excellent Trigg person was guiding them to Outerly in the context that the Zaubergers might end up there for life in what amounted to being a small palace . . .

The skimmer dipped gently into a vast vertical tube like the downgrade to Hell. Here Frey momentarily clasped the shoulders of his wife to infuse courage into her; and Freya thrilled, not because this indip was new, for they took it annually, but because the shoulder-embrace proved to her that Frey still wanted to protect her. Or was Frey merely hanging onto her to protect himself? They clung, as annually they did (for neither of them was a skimmer-driver) while Dino swung them into the downgravity slide which looked and felt like a tunnel from here to the antipodes. At their high velocity, the down-feeling persisted during perhaps an hour; whereafter it yielded to an *up*-feeling. The shift was familiar to them, but for Freya it never ceased to be out-of-this-worldly— particularly at the run's midpoint here occurring, three thousand kilometers from their start, when, after a period during which falling seemed to have ceased and they were semi-floating, they began to rise, without any directional change. The experience was bizarre even for Kolly who understood the reasons.

"I never could comprehend this," Freya whispered to her husband—who answer-spat: "For the love of Hestung, how many times do I have to remind you? we've just passed through Critical Gravity!" Mentally, Freya punched her own little receding chin for asking him; she'd learned long ago that every question would earn her a kick in her ego; questions she shouldn't ask, not of Frey; if she would ask him no questions at all only part of the time would she make a mistake that would get her soulclobbered. She wondered why in hell *she* didn't ever clobber *his* soul for *his* rotten mistakes.

Dino turned all the way around to them, which a driver could safely do in this tube where all cars drove themselves. He said with sympathy: "I don't fault you for your confusion, Freya; I always feel it even though I know the answers. Maybe I can help you with a new way of looking at it. You comprehend that Hudibras is like a ball with a hollow center?"

"Yes—" Freya knew that Frey was watching her sardonically; but with Dino's luminous eyes upon her, for once Freya didn't care. (Kolly was perceiving most of this.)

"All right," Dino proceeded. "Now: all the mass of the Hudibras-ball is in its shell-thickness between the outside and the central hollow. Got that, Freya?"

"Well, yes—"

"One more thing. *Down* means, toward gravity's pull; *up* means, away from it. In your central hollow called Innerly, gravity is pulling you toward the outside of the world-ball, so *down* therein is the concave floor of the hollow. But on Outerly, everything seems magically turned inside-out! There, gravity is pulling you toward the *inside* of the ball; and *down* is the convex outer shell."

"It might even be," smoothly interposed Frey, "that somebody on Outerly and somebody in Innerly are standing on the soles of each other's feet."

"Brilliant aperçu, Professor!" Dino bootlicked. "Now, Freya—in this tube, *down* from either outer or inner surface of the planet means *toward Critical Gravity*, which in turn means the spheroid stratum of maximum-gravity mass. When we started downtube from Innerly, we were heading *toward*

the Critical Gravity stratum, that is, down; but
now that we have passed through the stratum we
are heading *away* from it, or up. And when we
return to Innerly, it will be just the opposite. Got
it, Freya?"

"GOT IT!" Freya yelled. "Doctor Trigg, you are
absolutely GREAT!" She turned to her husband,
all set to demand: "Why didn't *you* explain it to me
that way?" but she cut it off. Stonily, Frey stared
forward uptube. Freya knew the expression: it
was poison. Oh, dear. Well, let it alone: the sepsis
of the moment might drain away.

Freya was considering Dino an absolute dear!
Why couldn't Frey be like that? Before their marriage, and for a while afterward, Frey had been
sweet—and then something had seemed to happen. After the first decade of patience, Freya had
come to understand that Frey's nastiness to his
little wife was not transient; but the habit of acceptance had set in, Freya couldn't fight it. And now
it had been *five* decades . . .

Recognizing Freya's feelings, Dino was irresistibly drawn to play with them eventually, just as an
incidental diversion from his main thrust. For now,
though—and with primacy, even during *any* incidental diversion—THE GALACTIC JET-SPUME!
Toward this end, Frey Zauberger's mind-and-
music-enslavement was centrally dynamic.

Vacationing year after year, the Zaubergers had
been repetitiously amazed by the outlandish magnificence of Outer Hudibras. No traffic conges-
tion here: wealth had built the highways, and only
wealth and select tourism used them. No man-
made drab out here, either: Outerly had been
mostly left alone in its natural wild, snow-capped
mountains and all.

Just here, they were running along a mountain

apron out of which the highway was tastefully carved. Stretches of thick twisty-tree forest, curtaining sight of ocean which they could hear on their left (but sometimes remotely below) alternated with multikilometer squares of meadow-plateau. Sun. Skyblue. Birds (inferior to *Garbans*, being fliers) . . . Just for this while of reverent silence, Frey and Freya were close; but ironically, neither of them felt it, so rapt were they in the gigantic mysteries of outer-planetary nature.

As to Hudibras' outer world, lots of Innerly folk, perhaps a large majority, stayed uninterested, desiring to avoid the ravages of agoraphobia. The Zaubergers, blessed with clean absence of that, always came outside with exultation (which, in Freya's case, was timid and even a bit guilty).

Leaving them with it, Dino concentrated on driving and on mental weaving. He was maximizing the scenic drama of their approach. He had Croyd to ruin.

Taking a byway, they darted left then right to run along a narrow dirt road with portside ocean in unobstructed view. Here Dino lowered three wheels out of the skimmer body and switched-off the elevator air-jets; otherwise, they would have choked on dust, losing view of the ocean and everything else.

The Zaubergers, Kolly noted, were immersed in oceanizing, particularly inhaling the most magical of all Outerly magics brought to sharp point as one gazed at water (large bodies of the stuff!) exhibiting a spherical convexity which outraged sensory habits nurtured in concave Innerly planetary surface—a convexity complete with horizoning beyond which sailing things gradually appeared upward or disappeared downward.

Entering a village whose unexpectedly dingy buildings (among Outerly folk, dinginess could sometimes be *in*) cut off their ocean view, they pulled up in front of a particularly drab two-story weathered-timber structure. "Out all passengers!" Driver Dino sang; and, having assisted Freya out of the car, he led her into the building, with bemused Frey and Kolly at their heels.

They ascended a long steep flight of straight-forward wooden stairs: no landings, just step above step. At stairtop, Dino turned right, ushered them a short distance down a narrow corridor, swung left, and conducted them through an undistin-guished door. Beyond the door, a down-stair con-fronted them; Dino descended, his passengers descended; at stairfoot, they passed through still another door

and unaccountably emerged upon a semi-high place: no floors, no walls, no roof: en-tirely outdoors, but with nothing special to be seen left or right or forward. Dino uttered: "Be alert, now—we are on the threshold!" and he drew them forward, with confused Freya on his arm and Frey abreast of them on the other side of Freya while Kolly eagerly followed, until the side-walling folia-tion of this trail fell theatrically away and Dino, pointing left, cried: "LOOK!"

Look indeed! They were gazing from a true high place across an ocean bay, and the far bayside was was picture-filled by what Frey saw/felt as

pale blue sky-cyclorama centered on an imperfectly sug-gested white unCrested Crest-cross whose elon-gate lower stem downfingered without touching it a spreading

low varicolor-tourmaline mansion broad-reclining on sharp shards of icy-white ala-baster floating eternally fixed in liquid turquoise

Frey whispered: "You conceive that *this* is—for *me?*"

Replied Trigg: "Conceivably."

Freya expostulated: "It *can't* be! it just *can't*—"

Swinging on her, Frey bellowed: "What in Untergaard does *can't* mean?"

"What indeed?" cooed Dino (but the distant palace was only an instrumental aspect of his reference). "Let's get back to the skimmer and *go* there."

Their skimmer (whose wheels had vanished at a new incursion of pavement) halted, when shadows were long, beside a noble gateway of wrought marodion; beyond the wall, a hint of the majestic manse extruded itself into visibility out of an arborescent-foliaceous copse. Deploying a remote-control device, Dino swung inward-open the gates. The invaders penetrated the private forest, their elevation gently rising all the time, until they stopped near a singularly undistinguished masonry stair; here Dino cut the engine, and the skimmer soughed to the ground. "All out here!" he lilted, dismounting and going back to help delicate little Freya down. "I could have brought you in by the grand entrance, but this private postern has charms of its own. Forgive me if I precede you, for guidance and for safety."

He led them up the time-rotted-and-patina'd stairway, here where twilight was shadowed into dusk; the stair was dank and precarious, the steps and the walls were mossy-slippery stones which often wobbled, and there was no handrail. "In fact," he commented, "there is a fine stressed-calumnion handrail, so valuable that I have hidden it; but if you buy, I will restore it." Eager Frey was mounting just behind him, having thrust Freya back so that she had to balance herself, with Kolly below-rear ready to catch Freya if necessary.

Reaching stairtop, they debouched upon a house-encircling veranda whose floor was slabbed blue slate and whose waist-wall seemed nondescript in twilight. Following the course of this terrace, they circled manse-end until, rounding a sharp curve, they found themselves at manse-front

"GREISSHEIST!" swore Frey, stopping dead; and the two women, coming up to him, filled their lungs audibly. All the ocean lay below and beyond, with the westering sun sinking into her to create a watery gold fingerblaze crossing ocean and laying a dull-radiant fingertip on the manse-front. The opulent low light illuminated this facade, gilding the varicolor tourmaline which constituted the veranda's outer walling. Frey stepped quickly to the waist-high wall to peer downward at the sharp shards of alabaster on which the manse was founded, seeming to float on the ocean which then had been turquoise but now (except along the ruddy suntrack) was indigo . . .

Dino insisted that Frey play host at an opulent dinner in the dining hall whose vaulting was lofty and whose appointments were delicately luxurious. Frey sat proudly at the head, and Freya confusedly at the foot, of a table four meters long and indefinitely extensible; precisely two meters from either end, Dino and Kolly faced each other across the table's two-meter width. There were a waiter named Neunbals and a busboy named Tenpinz whose countenances and motions were unusual and whose arms were suitably long.

When all was downed, Dino personally served a brandy whose bouquet wafted them heavenward; and he suggested that they enjoy their liqueurs in the music room which, until now, the Zaubergers had not seen. He caused Frey, with Freya on his arms, to precede him and Kolly thither. They passed through a low doorway . . .

"HAUGENLAUGEN!" roared Frey, mule-halting; and once again frightened Freya sucked in breath. This parquet-floored music room, whose area was perhaps three hundred square meters, was in all respects the ultimate in high baroque, almost grotesque in its wall-and-door inlaying of gold and ivory. Every piece of furniture was an obviously authentic example of that centuries-ago period when the nobles of Outer Hudibras had celebrated grace, gallantry, villainy, and the muses while the middle classes were burrowing into Innerly. High above, the ceiling carried the baroque motif to Faustian infinitude in a many-plied complex of submarine curvatures and trompes l'oeil at whose deep centrality an irregular semidome of profound blue suggested no ceiling at all but only space. (Kolly yearned toward that ceiling.)

"BLAUFLAULAU!" howled Frey. "Freya, *look!*" Gripping both his wife's right arms, he was two-arm pointing obliquely upward with his pointy arms-and-fingers quivering stiff like those of an excited child. At the room's focus of highest interest, perhaps four meters above the floor hung a marble-railed balcony whose rail and whose twin approaching stairways curved to harmonize with the prevailing space-curvature; and rising above the rail was

but Frey, having forgotten Freya, was already up one of the twin curved stairways; and while fearful Freya upward watched, Frey settled himself onto the bench (with his back to the watchers below) and slammed thirty-six long fingers and toes onto the twelve keyboards of the mightiest ultrasynthesizer that any world had ever known. The resulting diapason ricocheted intricately in the convolutions of ceiling and walls and even furniture; catching this, Frey cut it off and listened to the residual echo—short-hit it again, cut it, listened—leaned on it prolongedly, now requiring his ears to listen more to the echoing than to the direct sound—galvanized his antennae into a dancing among stops while holding one complex dissonant chord and listening for the echo-variations—positioned a system of stops with his antennae and held them constant while first varying the chordation and then running into a rambling staccato fugue, attending to the echoes . . .

Cut!

. . . Swung himself off the bench, lurched to the balcony rail, gripped it, peered breathless down not at Freya or Kolly but at Dino whose arm Freya was now clutching with four hands, felt his own lack of breath and began breathing deeply until he was able to talk, barked down at Dino: "HOW MUCH?"

Blandly Dino counter-queried: "How much *what?*"

"How much *money,* for the love of Heldenlieger! What the devil is your *asking* price for this joint?"

"What the *devil,* you say?" Dino frowned at the infernal implication; then Dino remembered his tactical program and named a price beyond prices.

Downstaring, Frey digested it, paled, began to lean dizzily too far over the rail; Freya's multiclutch hurt Dino's biceps; Kolly yelped, "Professor, get hold of yourself!" Grasping the rail just in time, Frey rescued himself, studied himself, uttered white-weak: "But Doctor Trigg—that is a hundred times my annual retirement income including all royalties and interest—but I have *got* to *have* this *palace!*"

He uptold him: "There is a condition under which it might be done."

Ghastly Zauberger down-groaned: "Name it!"

"Tell me, Professor: could you swing a lifetime annual payment of—" After delay for suspense,

Dino named a revised figure that was all but microscopic.

Frey snarled: "Don't play games with me!"

"*Can* you swing it?"

"Of course I can! Any pauper could! It's too easy. Trigg! What's the catch?"

"Would you be willing to spend a little daily time playing and recording music of my own composing? I mean, my music is only linear themes—" Kolly murmured: "Jeoud!" Dino continued: "We would have to work together on developing the variations and orchestrations, but—would you?"

Having assimilated that, Frey sat heavily down on the bench. In a strangulated voice: "What if I find that I simply hate your music?"

"I understand hate, Professor—oho, do I understand it! But perhaps you won't hate it. And in any case, two or three hours daily during at most a month should do it. After that—no obligation except the nominal annual mortgage payment, so highly do I value my themes and your elaborative executions."

"You are saying that for the silly little annual figure which you named, and for maybe a hundred hours of playing your music on this divine instrument, I can be lord of this manor during all the remaining years of my life?"

"For that price, my friend, and just this small bit more. I will need to approve your development of my themes, so you must permit me to be here whenever I choose, and you must not interfere with anything I do here. But I promise to maintain my own apartment in a secluded part of this house, and you will be unaware of me except during my music times with you."

Frey, standing now and leaning forward on the rail, down-husked: "Only that, and it's all mine— ultrasynthesizer and all?"

"Only that, and it's all yours," Dino upward-assured him. Dino's arm was now around Freya's waist; neither stricken Freya nor transfigured Frey appeared to be noticing.

Frey Barrymore-surrendered: "Done! What must I sign in my blood?"

"Done indeed!" sang out Dino, and he could feel Freya shuddering. "No signing, Frey; no blood. All our conversation has been flaked, Captain Kedrin here will add her vocal witness to the flake, I will give you a copy, and all that is legal enough on Outerly. Stay there: let me bring you a few samples of my theming, now that the agreement is already sound-sealed; and I do feel that you won't find the samples disagreeable to work with.

8. Repose at Zaubergerschlöss

The samples of Dino's musical theming captivated Frey by stimulating high-intensive concentration-pressure. Most of these experimental themes were linear-simple yet extremely rapid, entailing labyrinthine series of cadenza-variations using only the seventeen-note scale spanning several octaves. But every so often came a surprise: a veritable loop-the-loop in the music, which would encourage Frey's elaboration to skitter over multiple keyboards before settling back for a while into the linearity. Every note was staccato-distinct from all others: no ligatures, no slurs—although an untrained ear might seem to hear slurring because of velocity, just as a strip of distinct cinema frames generates an illusion of continuous movement. Delicious embroidery-potential! Why, performing such unusual studies would be *fun!* Frey was *cheating* Trigg! What a *miraculous* retirement!

At Dino's urging, Frey decided to forget Innerly on the spot, remaining here tonight and permanently. (The day would soon come when Frey would be desperately of two minds about this decision.) Dino promised to move everything in the Zauberger apartment out here; that same night, he brought off this transfer by teleportation.

In bed, Freya touched a Frey-shoulder and timidly whispered: "Honey, do we *really own* this magnificence? are you sure he hasn't somehow trapped us?"

Frey growled: "I keep telling you that Trigg and I have it all figured out. Why don't you *trust* me for a change, you dumb doxy? Go to sleep."

Long-and-often-lacerated Freya shrugged and turned away from her trenchant mate. Drowsily she reflected that after all she *was* as inferior as he kept saying she was; faith in him was the best way, probably. But until she went unconscious, fear about the life-change persisted; and in sleep, she tiptoed with foreboding before a certain door behind which must surely lurk a horror.

Turning away from his wife, Frey for a little while fell into the futility of wishing that he had tried to reassure her rather than swatting her. But soon Frey was able to terminate that silliness by reminding himself that he had to stay on top if their marriage was to keep succeeding. During decades with Freya, hadn't Frey established that this was the best formula in this man's world wherein wives kept deploying their feminine-emotional wiles to insinuate themselves into marriage-mastery? With that issue mentally settled for now, Frey drifted off into dreaming suffused with the golden joy of personal and social grandeur among the noble peers of Outerly.

"Dino—"

"Kolly?"

"Are you going to sleep, there?"

"No."

"Will you be kissing me soon?"

"No. Not tonight. I have to think tonight."

"What about?"

"Progress. Go to sleep."

"Don't you want my comments?"

"Not tonight. Tomorrow, maybe. Go to sleep."

"But—"

"*Go!*"

He was doing what he had taught and disciplined himself to do: lying in a species of relaxation which was the resting-equivalent of sleep but was not sleep, review-integrating projects with progress—on The Project, in this instance.

Inwardly he preened himself on his exquisite organization of psychic and cosmic factors: it counted as creativity, really it did, even though his creativity was meant to destroy. Already he had charisma-enslaved Kolly, thereby acquiring himself the *Sterbenräuber* as a handsome and spatio-temporally multipotent vehicle, and had bribe/charisma-enslaved Frey Zauberger, thereby acquiring himself the perfect cosmic stimulus-injector. The ensuing steps were radiant with audacity, clarity, and promise.

How glowingly had his horizons expanded since he had encountered that supra-Dino who called himself Darkside!

Kolly was purring a ladylike snore, agreeably and soporifically soft. Perhaps he would take her with him tomorrow, on the spatiotemporal scouting aimed at verifying that the theories on which his anti-Croyd plot was based did indeed apply, here among the Magellanic Clouds: his well-grounded and partially established theories related to galactic mantles, galactic fountains and jet-spumes, and the time-trace dynamics which that excellent Darkside had accepted under the acronym NORAP for Nodes of Rejected Alternate Possibilities.

He envisioned a helpless Croyd trembling with anger and frustration. *Good father Croyd*, he mind-murmured, *eat your heart out: your galaxy is doomed, and you will witness its demise.*

Did he mind-hear an exultant tenor *Yea verily?*

"Darkside," he whispered, not to awaken Kolly, "I smell doubt in your mind-voice, and I advise you to quench every doubt, lest you end by feeling foolish. Up and out will go the Zauberger music, cosmically out, along all-but-instantaneous iradio gradients which I will have preestablished. So easily, so very easily, am I initiating the prelude to Gotterdämmerung!"

8. Meanwhile, Elsewhen

Croyd, temporarily released now from routine galactic duty, was pursuing special emergency galactic duty—seeking Dino Trigg, who had abandoned Nereid and his galaxy in a mood of vengeful frenzy and was mentally, emotionally, and psycho-physically capable of anything at all, good or evil. With heart-hurt, Croyd was expecting evil; and it had to be headed off, or the galaxy would suffer, perhaps fatally.

Only, how would one go about finding Dino? The chances of him being at any specific point in germinal space could be expressed as one in $pi\ r^3$; in view of the time that had elapsed since his departure with *Sterbenräuber*, and in view of the ship's known maximum acceleration, r could be set at a maximum of 8×10^5 light-years—which amounted to a spatial volume of 25 million cubic light-years. In such an astronomical volume, the chances of randomly locating Dino, a mere spatial point, were practically infinite. But it was worse than that: because Dino was able and crafty enough to do his maneuvering in uptime (the specious past), it was necessary to factor-in *all time*; and now the chances against finding him *were* infinite.

It followed that Dino Trigg, who had departed in a mood of malevolence, must be quietly fertilizing-and-hatching his plans in a locale that was unfindable by randomly chosen search-methods. But he *must* be found! Could reason help?

Croyd thought it might, within limits. There was, however, an obvious need to start with a raw hound-dog tracking.

Every event in any present time develops out of an event that preceded it, and that prior event out of a prior event, and so on. As a series of events futurizes, each new event thrusts its line of ancestral events into uptime; and such event-lines, or traces, are indestructible. If Croyd therefore should invade uptime—"go into the past"—by just a few days, to the moment when despairing Dino had pushed off into space in a suicide try, Croyd could follow Dino's time-track, accelerating Croyd's tracking faster than the speed of the original Dino-track formation, until Croyd would catch up with Dino *now*, wherever and whenever Dino now might be.

Dino, nearly a week ago, was poised on a Nereid docking platform for his suicide leap into Neptune-space. This time, Croyd stood immediately behind him. It was Dino's past observed in Croyd's present; Croyd was sentient, but the rigidifying traces of Trigg were no longer so.

As Dino flexed for the death-leap, Croyd mounted him and clung to his back: the Old Man of the Sea with Sinbad; thus Croyd hurtled into space with Dino. Croyd was fully experiencing all the current experiences of the disaster-depressed Trigg-mind; while the Dino Trigg whose back Croyd embraced was experiencing nothing any longer, being a mindless organization of bygone time-tracks.

So mounted, Croyd was able to see what Dino had seen and feel what Dino had felt, precisely as Dino had seen and felt. He mind-heard himself mind-calling to Dino, and bitterly he felt the angry rejection by Dino. And then, in time's fullness, in the beginning terminal enfeeblement of Dino's asphyxiation . . .

Croyd, in Dino's brain-traces, heard and saw Darkside.

Although, as Croyd had indicated to Tannen, Croyd knew that Dino had an alter ego with whom Dino held imaginary conversations to assist his own thinking process, this was Croyd's first sight of projected Darkside. Certainly Dino's double did closely resemble Dino himself—and certainly, seen and heard via the Trigg sensorium, Darkside appeared absolutely real! Just for an instant, Croyd detached himself from the Trigg-brain long enough to look directly at Darkside: the image had vanished; but still through Dino's brain the phenomenon was real and vital . . .

Darkside *and* Dino unexpectedly vanished, leaving Croyd floating alone in uptime Neptune-space—and leaving no trace of themselves.

Vexed at the escape, Croyd comprehended what must have happened. He had taught Dino about *nontime*; and in this last-ditch oxygen-emergency, Dino-Brightside-and-Darkside had remembered and had gone there. And just as running water, entered by a fugitive animal, foils pursuers by obliterating the spoor of the hunted one, so nontime, in which uptime traces do not form, had cut off Dino's track.

Croyd might have entered nontime to pursue Dino—but to what end? since nontime, or non-spacetime, is an infinitely extended noncontinuum of unformed potentials: in nontime, Dino could be instantly anywherewhen. Which put Croyd right back to the point of his initial frustration.

Where now to turn?

Wait, now. *Sterbenräuber* . . .

Oho! there was *another* tracking approach!

GALAXIES IN DEEP SPACETIME

10. Two Billion Years Ago—NOW!

After an elegant breakfast outdoors on the ocean-side terrace (for Frey and Freya simply could not get enough of Outerly's fresh air and fantastic horizon), Dino stuffed the Zaubergers with instructions about their new castle; Neunbals, who was present, would relay all that was needful to Tenpinz whose structure was simpler but more muscular. Kolly was confused when Dino announced that he would leave the skimmer at Frey's disposal (Neunbals could drive, too); but Dino gave Kolly reassurance that Flaherty could "pluck us from our castle eyrie." In the event, Dino took Kolly out onto the high balcony of their tower apartment and simply teleported both of them into Flaherty's interior.

In space, en route to *Sterbenräuber*, he conducted a three-way conference with Flaherty and Kolly. He opened with a brief review: "Good Flaherty, I seem to remember that you can tempigate independently between twenty-five centuries earlier and twenty-five later than zero-level, which is the time-level wherewhen you are released from our mother ship. Correct?"

"Aye aye, sir," answered the crooning voder.

"Good, in a limited way. Now. Captain Kedrin,

as the skipper of *Sterbenräuber*, tell us how deeply she can plumb uptime."

"Minister Trigg, our ship is rated for 920 millennia, and she can push it a bit deeper." Kolly was proper-prim: Flaherty didn't need to know a damn thing about her personal life. (Flaherty, as it happened, wasn't programmed to care.)

Distressingly, Dino was nettled. His paired hands intertouched fingertips, and his head drooped so that the longest fingertips were supporting his chin just below his pursed lower lip.

The silence, awkward to Kolly, was neutral to Flaherty.

Dino announced: "The kind of time-depth which I require is more on the order of two billion years. *Two million* millennia."

There followed a silence of gradual sinking-in and consequent shock on the part of Kolly. (Flaherty's brain commented privately to Flaherty, TILT! and went on hold.)

Said Dino: "Flaherty, proceed to the mother ship, enter, and rest. By the time I reenter you, I will have thought of something."

Kolly took *Sterbenräuber* all the way down to her rated maximum of 920,000 years into the past of the Lesser Magellanic Cloud. "Shall I push for more?" she queried.

"Forget it," Dino told her; "another few thousand millennia would be a spit in the temporal ocean. From here, I can work with Flaherty—so anchor herewhen."

Somewhat later, having left the yacht in charge of Commandroid Myco, they reentered Flaherty and were injected into uptime space. Kolly, dying to know how *and why* Dino proposed to go two billion years deeper into uptime, was too intelligent to ask; for when he would be ready, he would be talking.

And he lost no time in saying part of it. "Flaherty, it is time for us to do a two-billion-year time-dive. Are you ready?"

"Oh, *yes*, sir!"

"But, Flaherty—*can* you do it?"

"Oh, *no*, sir."

"And why not, pray tell?"

"Because, sir, I have no gauges for it."

"But do you know how it *feels* when you time-dive?"

"Oo, yeah!"

"On my signal, then, get that feeling while *I* do the diving."

"You, sir?" Flaherty marveled. Kolly was enthralled.

"Just keep remembering this, good Flaherty: no matter what may happen, you have to keep me inside of you, and you have to stay with me to keep me from getting out of you. That will require you to dive with me as deeply as I do—and Captain Kedrin will take upon herself the job of staying with us. Got it?"

"Care for a printout, sir?"

"No. If you think you understand me, say aye aye, sir."

"Aye aye, sir."

Kolly interjected: "And how am *I* supposed to manage the staying with you?"

"Just exist, Kolly: you are already Flaherty-contained, you will automatically stay contained. Flaherty, consider *time* itself: do you know what time *is*?"

"Nay nay, sir."

"Fine; no more do I. Ready?"

In the course of her uptiming, the *Sterbenräuber* had made a drastic and swift lateral move in space, to a position completely outside the Lesser Magellanic Cloud.

From this viewpoint, not only was Lesser viewed whole with Greater beyond, but also Least, the third cloud invisible from Erth, could be partially descried between Lesser and Greater.

Now also noticeable was a sort of glowing and partially starred ribbon or sweeping mantle between Greater and the others, as though at some time in the past the two smaller clouds had broken away from Greater and moved away leaving behind them a trail of stardust. Generally accepted theory held that precisely this had happened some two billion years in the past. Dino was about to verify that theory in the process of verifying some other cosmic theories—and weaving all of them into explosive pattern.

Something else was visible when you viewed the three clouds in transcolor as Flaherty and Dino and Kolly now did. What they now perceived in arousing color-drama were three *galactic ion-fountains* in hyper-energized upward-downward play, one arising out of the heart of each Magellanic Cloud, fed by and reenergizing the ionic mantle that cocooned each galaxy. In columns of blue-hot plasmic flow, the fountains ascended tens of thousands of light-years into intergalactic celestiality, while in-between columns of somewhat cooler red-hot gas descended back into the mantles. In her stirred fancy, Kolly could imagine the ferocity of the supernova explosions, about one per century per galaxy, which powered the spectacular eruptions and therefore wove the transcolor-glowing cocoons.

Dino murmured: "Kolly, have you experienced transcolor displays before this one?"

"I should hope so! They've been around since the twentieth century, haven't they?"

"Not quite. Way back then, what they used was called *false* color; it was added by computer to telemetrically transmitted unicolor photos. But our transcolor is direct imagery with the human visual range expanded to embrace a far wider spectrum of frequencies, enabling us to see these ionic mantles and fountains just as we *really* would see them if our naked eyes could accept a wider range of light-colors . . . But that's enough theory for now. Flaherty?"

"Sir?"

"Be good enough to approach the clouds in such a way that their images on your major viewscreen will be as follows: they will almost fill your screen both laterally and vertically, including the fountains, yet each of the three clouds will continue to be visible."

Having executed, Flaherty queried: "Shall I hold this position, sir?"

"Hold relative spatial position only, while we are changing temporal position."

Then, concentrating on continuance of his enwrapment by Flaherty, Dino time-dove. Or, in another phrasing, perversely and with enormous energy expenditure he uptimed profoundly from the already deep uptime position of *Sterbenräuber*, moving up-current into remote past. And Flaherty did stay with him; and consequently, so did entranced Kolly.

The pastward-travel principle was simple enough, and Kolly had learned to understand it without comprehending it. Advanced tempigation theory was based on the analog that the passing of time (= the course of germinal development) generates an unending series of concentric event-spheres, with germinal actuality (= live events) constituting the outermost sphere; while the successively smaller spheres within it are serially older strata of the past, rather like the concentric growth-rings in a cross-section of a tree. Each physical event in its actuality spawns a descendant, perishes, and sinks into past. Necessarily, therefore, the magnitude of each past event shrinks as the fossil of that event sinks deeper.

Then if a germinal being (such as Dino or Kolly or Flaherty) can arrive at sinking into past *while maintaining its own magnitude relative to the era of its own germinality*, it will find that past events shrink with respect to itself, shrink smaller and smaller at deeper and deeper time-levels.*

And of course there was no reason why Flaherty and its contained party should not maintain magnitude as they invaded the realm of shrinking past events; for the invaders themselves continued being germinal-actual.

The shrinkage phenomena were highly noticeable now in the viewscreens, as Flaherty sank or rose or whatever into the remote past. Relative to any viewscreen, the Magellanic Clouds were degrowing smaller. They maintained their bright images, which seemed to imply one of three alternatives about light-propagation in uptime: either light-propagation continues although all other matter is frozen, or light too is frozen and Flaherty was merely registering photons which happened to be frozen *there*—or something different from either.

Since Flaherty possessed no deep-range time-gauge, only wild guesses could be made about the number of years or lifetimes by which Dino's current past-invasion should be measured, now that the galactic images had been reduced until they occupied only a quarter of the prime viewscreen. Trigg's feeling was, that the temporal depth was not yet enough; so his time-dive continued, with sexless Flaherty jealously enwombing him.

---

*A curious reader may find an exception in *The Rape of the Sun*.

Minutes . . .

The triplex Magellanic Clouds now appeared larger than one bright star among many stars. Dino barked: "Cut pastwarding!" Therethen they were, with Kolly marveling. "We're getting there," he told Flaherty. "Center the nebulae on your prime screen, then move in until the screen barely includes all three galactic components, then set yourself to hold that special position and report."

Screen-maneuverings; then a stable positioning. "Done," said Flaherty, "but we seem to have lost a galaxy." In fact, although Greater stayed intact, the backtiming process had re-fused Lesser and Least: again they were one. Just now, in the holographic imagery, the two clouds overlapped but were distinctly separate, with Greater continuing to be larger than Lesser even in close perspective; and the starry dispersal-trail between them was gone.

Kolly uttered: "How time-deep, do you think?"

"More than a billion years," Dino ventured, "on theoretical considerations; but we aren't there yet. Flaherty, here we go again; keep containing me." He reentered the time-dive, pressing downward or upward or whatever into still deeper past, continually watching the screen.

The two galaxies, momentarily enlarged by Flaherty's closer approach, now steadily shrank again—and, diminishing, approached each other more and more nearly—until they were like a silver half-credit and a silver quarter-credit, still overlapping laterally and, in the hologram, just barely separate in depth, prevented from coalescing into each other only by the ferocity of their outward momentum imparted by the Big Bang billions of years earlier. And yet it was frozen momentum: in uptime, only germinal invaders like Dino can move. (Croyd had often wondered aloud, in Dino's presence, whether it was uptime that Parmenides had in mind with his changeless universe—or Einstein with his four-dimensional universe wherein every change was a point on a changeless worldline.)

Again Dino had Flaherty approach the twin galaxies until they filled the prime viewscreen. Again they time-dove—until—

"There, now!" Dino breathed; and a little exclamation came out of Kolly. For, all of a sudden, the Greater and Lesser Clouds had back-coalesced into a single galaxy which spurted, not mere fountains, but a frighteningly exquisite jet-spume.

"It is," announced Dino, "as we have long suspected; but until now there was no way to verify it with eyeball finality. At a very early time in the history of the Magellanic Clouds, the time-level which we are now visiting, these galaxies were altogether a single galaxy. But they had originated as separate galaxies; and therefore, when partially random physical forces pulled-and-drove them together, Greater cannibalized Lesser; and the result was the jet-spume that you now see. It continued to spurt for God knows how long; but then somehow, in some catastrophic convulsion, the single galaxy was torn into three. And that was the end of this magnificent jet.

"Kolly, Flaherty, this galactic jet is what we are going to use as the destroyer of all civilization *and the possibility of civilization* everywhere in Croyd's beloved Sol Galaxy!"

Kolly chilled—and yet, somehow, she also thrilled; no part of her mind suggested that Dino needed slow killing. She feebly remonstrated: "But the jet is long dead—"

"There are ways," Dino declared, "of revitalizing it; and Zauberger's music, correctly deployed, offers us one such way.

"Flaherty, move in on the galaxy."

*   *   *

When Flaherty halted, announcing "Sir, I am one meter off," in the viewscreen the pastward-recoalesced Magellanic Cloud was no larger than a fishbowl with a jet-spume that vanished far above the screen. Dino made sure that the screen was adjusted to reflect accurate size without magnification or reduction; then he stood gazing at the image and rubbing hands together.

Here among the galaxy's deep uptime trace-filaments, had Roboat Flaherty kept moving forward until the roboat would feel contact, Flaherty would never have *felt* this contact, but would have kept moving forward until the galaxy would have been behind Flaherty—for the galaxy would have passed cleanly through Flaherty and passengers. What looked like a tiny galaxy was really a screen-image of rigidified nuclear traces, of filaments extending from origin to germinality; so thin were these filaments that one of them could slice through a quark without troubling that microparticle one little bit. Slender filaments, yes; yet so massive in terms of inertial mass were those fibers, that nothing germinal could be as massive. Consequently, nothing germinal could budge those fibers—and only germinality has physical power. Hence, even the chromatic jet was unchangeably immobile at any given uptime-moment; it might as well have been a marble sculpture.

(Dino avoided remembering that it was Croyd who had taught him all this.)

He inquired of Flaherty: "Can you remember the feeling of this time-depth?"

"Clearly, sir; the feeling is RAM-clear and even subconsciously ROM-latent."

"For retrieval, label it two billion years negative in ITC units. Do you think that, without my guidance, you can return accurately to this wherewhen?"

"Yo."

"Could you station other roboats down herewhen, and variously between herewhen and the germinal time-surface, and command them under me?"

"Yes. We all have compatible systems."

"Could you communicate your feeling of this time-depth, along with the indexicals, to the master computer on the *Sterbenräuber,* so that *Sterbenräuber* could achieve this time-depth accurately in the absence of appropriate gauges?"

"I could indeed, sir, sir, sir."

"Why three sirs?"

"In my engrossment with the problem, I had missed two."

"I relieve you from ever hereafter saying sir."

"Why, sir? did I do something wrong?"

"No, you did not; it is only my whim."

"Sir, what is a whim?"

"Just keep on sirring me. A question occurs: how can you know that I am a sir and not a ma'am?"

"Sir, they built into me an intuition bank for sexual discrimination, whatever that may mean, sir."

Bizarrely, Dino informed Kolly that he was about to depart Flaherty for an uptime space-walk; she could join him if she chose. She chose. He cautioned her to suit up with special care and to carry as many hours of oxygen as Flaherty's store of life-support packs could afford her. While she was suiting up, he simply undressed.

Naked except for a throat-mike, carefully he said: "Flaherty, I have certain precise instructions for you; and if you don't entirely understand them, it is essential that you keep asking questions until you do. The first instruction is, that Captain Kedrin and I are about to depart your interior, but we will return after a few hours of exterior scouting."

"Sir, I am confused, sir. I thought I was to keep
you inside of me no matter what might happen.
Well, what is happening is, that you are now or-
dering me to let you out of me; but am't I even so
supposed to keep you inside of me—sir?"

Requiring his temper to stay even, Dino purred:
"Good thinking, Flaherty, and you are now at
least one sir ahead. Your confusion results from a
fault of mine at the start of this, I should have
forewarned you that my orders to you would be
changing about now. If you wish, we can go back
to the time-point just before I gave you that direction, and I can say it again with amendments."

"Wouldn't that be a lot of trouble, sir?"

"It would indeed, indeed."

"Then let's don't. In return, I will stop calling
you sir, usually. I will enter in my stipulative bank
that you originally meant to say the order with
your present emendations. I now understand that
I am to let you go outside of me. But this time it
would be wise for you to be very explicit indeed.
Can you now give me the whole program?"

"How many megabytes can you remember and
manipulate?"

"Sir, seven to the eleventh power."

"It is a fine crap-shooting number, Flaherty, but
it is too thin for my whole program. Accept this
much. When I want to go out of you, stay herewhen
and await my return. When I return, let me in,
and prepare for the next program-segment. Got
it?"

"Yo."

Under the primordial circumstances, Dino felt a
faint chill of hazard—and found it almost sensu-
ally arousing. He emphasized: "If I cannot return,
possibly Captain Kedrin can; and in my absence,
you are to take orders from her—"

She interposed a bite: "In your absence, Minister, Flaherty would do so anyhow."

"True, Captain; forgive my oversight. Anyhow, Flaherty: if neither of us returns, remain herewhen and await the return of one of us, even if it takes forever."

"What is forever?"

"Definable only by negations, now I think about it. So no matter how long we stay away, expect the return of one of us, and wait herewhen."

"I will be true, Minister, although I have never been informed how long it will take my memory to decay."

"Let us hope that it will outlast our absence. Ready, Kolly?"

"Ready." She was suitably suited; she wondered at his nakedness, particularly his unheadgeared head, but she asked no questions: Dino was Dino.

He said: "Now, Flaherty."

The boat replied: "Godspeed, then—whatever that is supposed to mean."

They were tethered to each other by a ten-meter kamatic field; but never did Kolly let them drift that far apart, despite the unpredictable alacrity of the Trigg space-swimming.

His exuberance propelled him through uptime-space in this profoundly past time-sphere which was contemporaneous with the origin of life on far-distant Earth. Immediately he thrust himself into the soul of the early-embryonic gas which was the borning galactic corona or mantle.

His exuberance wasn't blunting the point of his analytical exploration.

"Croyd," he remarked to Kolly through his throat-mike, "adores the sensation of swimming naked-free in space; and so would you, if it were possible for you." It was a satirical observation, a put-down both for Croyd and for Kolly. In the Trigg-mind, space-nakedness meant liberation from restraints to his practical progress; in the Darkside-motif, it was the only ecstatic way to go; and Darkside-haunted Dino could come to terms with it only with sarcasm which allowed him to be space-naked without seeming naïve. (Croyd needed no such tortuous self-justification, but Dino didn't appreciate this.)

Practical *progress?* toward galactic destruction? *progress?* Well; but isn't *progress* double-edged like a knightly sword and two-faced like Janus, so that it can proceed in any direction, toward good or evil or any interblend thereof?

Kolly, suited, minnow-swam in uptime infragas. That which Dino was exploring (using visual hypermagnification aided by brain-supplied transcolor) was a frozen kelp-forest of the ultrafine-ultramassive uptime-traces of gaseous events in past germinality, the eternally changeless debris of past presents.

There existed, however, a certain operation which could *supplement* the unchangeable forest with *new* germinality. Dino Trigg had developed the operational theory: it was what he and Darkside had called NORAP—Nodes of Rejected Alternate Possibilities. Dino had never applied the theory, but he had mathematized it and pseudo-tested it with computer simulations; and the ferocity of his thrusting for revenge on Croyd drove him recklessly now to depend on his theory and plunge into the main chance. And Croyd, in his knowledge of Dino's capabilities, would not have hesitated to bet on him—provided that Dino would have the will to go all the way with it.

Dino swam naked looking for NORAPs, and his brain-enhanced vision would detect their radiation if any were there. So aroused was he in this quest, that he kept running low on buttock-stored oxygen and having to refuel on Kolly's life-support pack (but there was plenty for both). Once, during a rest-pause, he briefed Kolly who, hypo-euphoric with the beginnings of deep-rapture, kept seeing an aureola around and above Dino's head:

"The trace-filaments of uptime," he reminded her, "are the serial fossils of microparticular moments piling one atop another like coral in a building reef. Generally, the traces are immutable and unmovable—with a subtle type of exception related to if-nodes."

"And if-nodes are—?"

"A NORAP or *if-node* occurs at each particle-instant when an individual particle might have moved in any one of several ways, but actually did move in just one of those ways, leaving one or more unexplored possibilities. Even at the level of complex and more-or-less intelligent creatures, whose uptime-traces are bundles of filaments like the multiple neurone-fibers in a spinal cord, compounded if-nodes occur in a bundle whenever the creature has chosen to do one thing when instead it might have done some other thing."

Well, then: Dino was seeking if-nodes in the infragas corona and in the central jet of the original, amalgamated Magellanic Cloud.

And he kept finding them!

And he knew that, given certain types of influencing forces, an if-node could be made to germinate into reality an *alternate developmental possibility*. This new-reified course of action could then be developmentally accelerated to compete with what was already in place.

Entranced Kolly queried: "*What* types of influencing forces?"

"Well, Kolly, just for instance: a hyper-intensive radiation bombardment, when the cyclical varia-

tions of the radiation are controlled by certain
planned patterns of ultra-high-velocity stimuli—
such as music."

Kolly didn't get it, but her own elation was too
high for studying it out or asking questions. Much
later, she would get thinking about it—and only
then would dismay set in.

Herenow, though, Dino was inwardly snarling:
"Croyd, whether your galactic civilization lives or
dies depends right now on my success or failure
with the music of Frey Zauberger!"

"Are you there, Minister, Captain?"

"Trigg answering. We are here, Flaherty. Were
you worried about us?"

"What is worry?"

"It is a condition of doubt coupled with an unfavorable feeling."

"I was worried. Will you return into me?"

"The captain and I are returning into you immediately. Then all of us will return into *Sterbenräuber*, and I will set things up for the operation I have in mind—an operation toward whose
success you are central."

"I am flattered, sir, ma'am, by your confidence.
Bill Bailey, won't you please come home?"

"Now where did you ever pick up *that*?"

"I heard you singing it on the way down—or *up*,
I think you said it really is."

"It really is neither, Flaherty. Temporal indexicals are not spatial directions."

"Sir, I *know* that!"

11. "Certain Planned patterns of Ultra-High-Velocity Stimuli"

In the Zauberger castle on Outer Hudibras, with steadily mounting euphoria, Dino kept feeding new musical themes to Frey. Above him beyond vision, the *Sterbenräuber* droned about in orbit, in process of being internally fitted with some sophisticated audio-amplification wiring, under the direction of Captain Kedrin whose irritation at Dino's protracted absences was impelling her toward an emotional brink.

Frey kept driving into the music, not two but twelve hours daily, taking rest-breaks only at the insistence of his music-master (who wanted to keep Frey fresh and psychophysically vigorous) or sometimes at the piteous importunings of Freya (who was soul-crawlingly afraid of the situation's demonism).

During such breaks, Dino would conduct Frey and Freya to a white-enameled wrought-durundium table on the veranda with the sea overlook; he would sit there with them while diminutive android Neunbals brought drinks and snacks. During such breaks, Frey kept hammering at Dino: "My God, man, I am running out of your themes!" (Dino continued learning that humanoids or hominids had, in their several tongues, God- or god- or totem-oaths on every planet where they had arrived or evolved.)

For a while, he was ready with new themes, having run off a lot of this quasi-genetic music (corresponding to sequences of amino acids in genes) aboard the *Sterbenräuber*. These themes he stored in his brain to regurgitate for Frey at will; but so swiftly did Frey convert Dino's barebone themes into richly ornate compositions, that the master had to hit the ship's computer again. Despite interruptive shipboard interludes with Kolly, who was beginning to bore him but whose servitude must be serviced, his growing urgency was keeping him sufficiently ahead of Frey.

Dino's days and evenings were not entirely worktimes. Frey knew how to relax over meals, and he taught his new music-mentor discreet relaxation-secrets (which had nothing to do with sex). Even his little wife Freya was losing some of her inferiority-tension and playing up to her two companions; she hoped that eventually she could once more be demonstrating, to Frey and to herself, her usefulness by doing the cooking and housework. But after most of a lifetime at that, Freya was for the moment content to be relieved by that excellent Neunbals—particularly since leisure brought ught her into more and more familiar contact with this admirable Minister Dino Trigg on whom Freya was developing something that resembled a crush.

During one or two days and nights per week, Dino was back aboard *Sterbenräuber*, to the delight and relief of Kolly whether she was working with him or abed with him. He had much to inspect, and the Kolly-body was the least of it. In the grinning breadth of the yacht, there was space for a high-energized rekamatic impulse to become hyper-energized by being pingponged back-and-forth from wingtip to wingtip, but a circular cycling for many-times-multiplied angular momentum would be far more effective. This they were achieving by a deployment of six roboats (petty-officered by Flaherty) in front of the yacht and behind it, making with the wingtips an eight-point pseudocircle; from a viewpoint of charge-acceleration, a true circle was achieved by putting a bit of english on each point-discharge. A cyclotronometer aboard this experimental yacht established the effectiveness of the technique: it raised a particle's kinetic energy by r^3 per cycle, and there seemed to be no end and indeed no taper-off to the increments.

There was, of course, no truly equivalent substitute test for the real McCoy: bombarding primitive galactic if-nodes two billion years old. And Dino didn't want to do test-partials on the archaically consolidated Magellanic Cloud, for fear of throwing something out of balance. Luckily, analogous approaches were conceivable. Far out on the periphery of the Greater Cloud, and two billion years deep in backtime, he found the start of a star which, millions of years later, had been gravitationally overwhelmed by a neighboring and slightly older star; so remote were these stars from his centers of intended action, that he felt he could safely play around with them. Downtiming *Sterbenräuber* (which Flaherty had well coached), with its roboat-satellites, to the spacetime locus of the later-unfortunate star, he surrounded it equatorially with his one-ship six-roboat task force, thrust the cyclotron into action, and (when the meter showed an adequate energy level) sprayed the star's if-nodes with the yacht's energy cannon. When he then downtimed a billion years, he found the sprayed star still alive and growing, while of the cannibal star there lingered no trace.

If, on a summer's day at the seashore, you have ever spent most of your swimming time under water, delighted and aroused by submarine scenes on the bottom and around and above you, then you can taste the subjectivity of Dino's repetitious uptiming. Even though Flaherty had, with entire fidelity and felicity, internalized his (its?) space-time coordinates and had correctly coached his (*his!*) brood, Dino Trigg trusted the accuracy of none of it. In his naked body The Master kept uptiming profoundly in order to spot check the positionings of the roboats and the adjustments of their new rekamatic fittings for receiving and transmitting and focusing Zauberger-music.

Compulsively Dino kept time-diving: to re-view the primitive Cloud-jet, to recheck the primitive Cloud-mantle, to be certain that both were there unchanged and ready for his if-node tampering. Toward the end of each heavenly break, he would fidget with unease: all the dispositions were perfect, the yacht and all the roboats were ready, Flaherty was the perfect petty officer—but what about the Hudibras connection? Grudgingly he would spend some sack-time with Kolly, because her illicit command of the *Sterbenräuber* made her his virtually indispensable instrument and required that she be kept in thrall. But early in the morning, he would be aboard Flaherty en route to the Zauberger castle, there to pass days and nights inspiring and critically auditioning Frey's musical output.

Between such frenetic yet studiously meticulous operations, Dino relaxed with the Zaubergers. And often, when Frey would go back to his ultrasynthesizer for another bout of swift-intricate genius, Dino would lead Freya away for one or another excursion out into the marvelous aromas and sights and sounds of this magical Outer Hudibrasian world.

Frey and Dino flake-recorded this music whenever a segment of it had attained a degree of perfection which *almost* satisfied both of them (for neither was capable of being totally satisfied about anything). In his off moments, Dino kept rerunning the stereoflaked progression of themes and variations; and if he was doing this for self-reassurance, it was working, because the Zauberger realizations of his intertwined gene-pattern scorings were Berlioz-fantastic-bombastic. He could not pretest the effectiveness of this music on a cosmic scale, somewhat as one cannot test the effects of a new missile-weapon on an enemy city for want of a war; but in terms of theory, content analysis, and his indirect uptime-testing of the interfaced cyclotron-cannon, the music was absolutely certain to work.

In the course of Dino's wanderings with Little Wife Freya, who so tenderly and curiously reminded him of his mother, it was inevitable that the Freya/Dino conversations should grow intimate. A time came when Freya, weary of being a soul-battered wife, having found finally a friend whom she could trust (and for whom, if Freya would admit it to herself, Freya was feeling the least little bit of desire), opened her heart to Dino about the tribulations of marriage with Frey. She summated: "Oh, Minister, I keep feeling so damn *inferior!*"

That was when Dino slipped his arm around Freya's waist for her comforting, here in the twilit woods where they wandered; and then they paused in their stroll, for Freya was pressing her head against Dino's upper arm (being too short to head-reach his shoulder) and was weeping bitterly. Dino held her, avuncularly of course; but in the solar plexus of Dino there stirred the piquant quivering that signified, not mere desire, but desire for conquest of what is morally off limits.

While he and Freya eased themselves back to the Zauberger castle, the Master's mind and heart and gonads were deliciously aswirl with a delectable side-project. Something like this was what he needed for his unwinding, after his prolonged fury-driving and immediately after he would have pulled the trigger of triumphant destruction.

Over dinner—where the three sat at two sides of the banquet-table center, with Dino facing the Zaubergers—Frey, dinner-dressed in an astonishingly feminine off-one-shoulder blouse (but with pants) which semi-revealed the breastless midridge of his avian chest, aroused the Master's enthusiasm by presenting to him, across table, a little pewteroid casket which was a flake-system depository. "Herein repose," Frey announced with god-pride, "our most recent collaborative compositions, all magnificent, my dear Dino, and all now recorded to my—well, perhaps not to my absolute satisfaction, since nothing I ever do attains perfectly to that standard, but at least, recorded so well that any small improvements I might make would inevitably be canceled by blurrings at some other points."

Dino accepted the casket with real emotion. He told Frey—contriving to include Freya in the communication and to huskify his voice a trifle—"My gratitude is greater than I can express. Dear Frey, you have discharged the major condition of our contract, leaving only the insignificant annual payments to make this castle yours in fee simple." The payments were silly, except that without them, Zauberger would have been motive-suspicious; just now, Frey was merely grateful.

Nevertheless, Frey drove it to the wall: "Ultra-synthesizer and all?"

Magniloquently he assured him: "Ultrasynthesizer and all, indeed!"

Freya injected: "But you didn't tell us how much fee simple we will also have to pay."

Frey scorned down upon her: "Fee simple means simple property, nitwit!" Beaming, he turned to Dino: "I am happier than you can possibly know. My only regret is, that there will be no more of your incomparable themes." He hesitated: "Or—*might* there be more?"

Having gazed ardently at doting Freya, Dino leaned toward Frey, engaging the musician's eyes. "Possibly so, depending on inspiration. Tell me, Frey Zauberger—you who must surely be wearied by your prolonged bout of high-pressure creativity—might you be tempted by a vacation offer?"

Frey narrowed his eyes. "A vacation? From all my new castle-splendor?"

Dino kept darting direct enticement-glances at Freya. "I mean, a vacation in deep space. We can travel in luxury whither you wish, from galaxy to galaxy should you desire that, aboard my yacht *Sterbenräuber*."

"That is the name of your yacht? How robustly romantic!"

"Is it not! And the high point of our vacationing will be, that you will be on hand when I broadcast your sublime conceptions into space—and with your own eyes, you will see their effect on the stars."

"Oh, heady, heady!"

"Freya must come along, of course."

Frey turned to Freya whom in fact he loved in Frey's peculiar way. On a shy nod from his wife, Frey turned upon Dino a gaze of resplendent radiance.

*   *   *

Aboard drone-orbiting *Sterbenräuber*, Kolly murderously paced the Operations Bridge. It was absolutely beyond doubt, now: Dino was using her, he had *always* been using her, he had lightly destroyed her career in order to use her, *she* had lightly destroyed *her own* career in order to *be* used by him; and now he was using Zauberger and without question was positioning himself to use that sweet little Freya, and the message from Dino that Flaherty had just relayed to Kolly made it clear that Dino was about to use Kolly to help him use Frey and Freya *right here aboard ship* . . .

"Captain."

Kolly froze in her tracks. That baritone voice . . .

"I spoke to you, Captain Kedrin."

Kolly swung to the squawk-box: that was the source, all right, but the voice . . . Getting control of herself, Kolly responded cold: "Skipper here. Who is calling?"

"Kolly, I think you know."

Good God, was Kolly had already? Taut she said: "I require that you identify yourself."

"That is prudent, Kolly; I could be a fake, you know. But I'm not. I am—"

"You are?"

"The voice of the ship's computer."

It was unnerving. "That is unlikely," Kolly managed; "the computer's voder is mezzo."

"That vocal timbre is internally adjustable. We'll quit the stretch-out, Kolly; you know quite well that I am Chairman Croyd."

The worst!

Kolly's legs weakened, and she sank into the President's chair. She deep-breathed three times. She enunciated: "Of course, Mister Chairman, I'll vacate your seat when you need it—"

The voder chuckled, and the chuckle destroyed Kolly. "Forgive me," said the voder almost sympathetically, "but the situation is faintly comical if you can look at it objectively. May I brief it for you, dear Kolly? Has anything like this ever happened before, do you think? You fell for a combination of charisma and hot sex. Believing that it was romantic love, you stole my ship and placed it at Trigg's disposition. And now, two things are catching up with you at the same instant: realization, and me."

Kolly downstared, thoroughly humbled, defeated, contrite, speechless.

"It appears to me," and now the voice had gone remorseless, "that you are thoroughly humbled, defeated, contrite, speechless. The last two conditions are appropriate, but the first two are not. You are an Astrofleet captain, Kolly Kedrin; it is inappropriate for you to be either humbled or defeated. Your comments?"

Up came Kolly's chin. "Mr. Chairman, I could deactivate the voder and the cabin-videoscan modules of the ship's computer. And I think that you could not stop me. Should I do so, I would no longer be humble or contrite, and you would be speechless and defeated."

"Very good, Captain. Are you going to try?"

"That depends on your attitude toward Minister Trigg."

"Toward Dino? It is an ambivalent attitude, Kolly. On the one hand, I cannot countenance either his hostility to his galaxy or the extravagance of this vendetta. On the other hand, apart from his vendetta, I love and admire him, and I am convinced that his outrageous change of attitude results from some weird mental trauma. Now you know my attitude. Will you now defeat and despeech me?"

Silence. Kolly was agonized; Kolly was pacing.

Warned the Croyd-haunted computer: "If you plan to continue your career in Astrofleet, then

Astrofleet now requires decisiveness. If instead you plan to continue in the service of Dino Trigg, scrapping your Astrofleet career, then the cause of Trigg now requires decisiveness. Kolly—sixty seconds."

Physically motionless Kedrin was mentally far-darting.

"Thirty seconds," asserted the voder.

Kolly swung to stare at the bridge-eye of the computer's cabin videoscan. "Request added time to discuss the consequent handling of Doctor Trigg."

"Request denied. Twelve seconds."

Outswung arms, upturned hand-palms: "I opt for Astrofleet, but I request judgmental fairness for Trigg."

Silence.

The computer said: "I applaud both your decision and your request, and so will Astrofleet. Kolly, confess that you've been had—and not by us."

Frowning down, Captain Kedrin enunciated with difficulty: "I have been had."

"Make a point of not being had again in that sense, Kolly; but I think you may have to let yourself be had again in another sense. It is crucial that we learn how far Dino will go with this before his conscience intervenes. It will serve all of us best if you will, until further notice, respond affirmatively to Dino's leadership and even to his domination no matter how shameful. Can you swing that, Captain?"

"No matter how shameful, Mr. Chairman?"

But a chime diverted Kolly's attention to one of the external visiphones. "Kedrin here," she responded, voice-activating a connection. Dino's face appeared on the screen, and Dino remarked: "I don't see anybody else on the bridge. Are we private, Kolly?"

"No body else is here," she truthfully told him; "you may speak freely."

Presently she knew that compliance with Dino's caprice was about to become shameful indeed. And she thanked any interested gods that she had the nerve and objectivity to see it through—and perhaps, with luck, even to enjoy it.

Croyd's control of the ship, whose computer he now inhabited, was fragmentary, beyond the voder and the audiovideo systems. It is one thing to command a computer objectively, making appropriate use of its responses: it is quite another thing to *be the mind* of a mighty computer, deploying it like a brain with a peripheral nervous system by intuitive empathy in order to make things happen just right throughout the body of a majestic and multipotentiary spacetime-ship and out among her satellite roboats. Even after many days of mental work in here, Croyd was still mind-performing much like a human infant finding its way around in its crib and among its toys; one difference was, that Croyd was bringing to the difficult project his intellectual-*obj*ective knowledge of what now he was teaching himself how to control *subj*ectively.

He could not yet fly the ship from inside her, or interfere with any physical mechanisms that Dino would be deploying, in the humanly-cosmically fearsome and loathsome business that Croyd was beginning to understand, without comprehending how Dino of all people could enter enthusiastically into such business.

But beyond gaining control of audiovideo and voder, he had made it a crash priority to master *Sterbenräuber*'s i-ray deployment—which gave her three external advantages: intimate and undetectable espionage, quasi-immediate mind-to-mind contact at a distance, and virtually instantaneous communication over astronomical distances.

[Readers eager to skip technicalities and get-on with the story are invited to omit the next two pages and pick-up events at that point . . .]

Croyd had theorized the i-ray possibility and had invented its techniques. His approach had begun by hypothetically denying what he called the *receptive or passive theory of vision,* which had been the dominant category of visual theory during at least nine centuries of evolving optical science, and which held that light-rays or photons reflected off illuminated objects enter the eye to create (with brain aid) visual experiences. In place of the receptive theory, he had tentatively substituted an *active-agent theory of vision*: that light impinging on a retina stimulates the retina (again with brain aid) to emanate i-rays, analogous to radar rays, which, on contacting an illuminated object, return almost instantaneous visual information to the source-retina.

Croyd had applied, to the two competing theories, the *full* Occam's Razor criterion: when two or more theories concerning phenomena account equally well for those phenomena, embrace the simplest theory.

Well: certainly the receptive theory was the simpler here, in that it required only one class of rays: those which were emanated from a star or another incandescent light-source, were bounced off the visual object (or rather, were partially absorbed by the object and then were emanated with altered frequency), and which thereafter found an eye.

On the other hand, this receptive theory did not happily explain certain visual phenomena not apparent to John Citizen. For example, you looked (with telescope or with naked eye) at a distant star; you saw, not merely a small fraction of the star, but the entire star (or one hemisphere, anyhow); yet, with emanations from separate points on the star-hemisphere diverging from each other as the square of the distance, only a tiny area of star-surface was what you *should* have seen. Croyd remembered a whimsy by post-medieval astronomer Arthur Eddington, who had satirically fantasied that among the diverging star-photons, one happened to hit an eye and cried out (approximately): "Hey, boys, here's an eye—let's all crowd in!"

Croyd had noticed that his active-agent i-ray hypothesis, while more complex, offered solutions to all visual problems solved by the simpler receptive theory, and also solved some others including Eddington's. If a stimulated retina should send out rays (refracted through the eye's lens) to the visual object, and then should bring back information (refracted through the eye's lens) to the originating retina, every phenomenal problem would be dissolved. Not only that, but the i-ray transit might be hypothesized as all-but-instantaneous; whereas the maximum speed of rekamatic propagation was 300,000 kilometers per second, which meant that under the receptive theory, all our visual information about a star or galaxy was outdated by at least four years ranging upward to billions of years.

So Croyd had tried it. And it had worked. This fact proved nothing one way or another about visual theory (or, as a necessary relatum, about camera-film theory), but certainly it was suggestive.

[End technicalities; back to the action . . .]

The important point here and now for Croyd's mind-espionage upon Dino was, that the *Sterben-räuber* carried i-ray equipment.

As the mind of the ship which was orbiting

Hudibras, Croyd now deployed his i-ray ground-reconnaissance capability to pick out the Zauberger castle and then, on the veranda, Dino who was promenading with his two birdy creatures. Upon him, Croyd zeroed in subjectively and intimately.

12. Darkside's Flip-Flop

After the Zaubergers had retired, Dino with heart joy-bursting mounted to his high place and gave rein to solitary exaltation. Safely invisible on the balcony of his private apartment in the tower, he stiffened his back and the rearwards of his thighs as he leaned on the rail with his moon-illumined hair back-blown by the wind that angered the night-sea far below. He rigidified his wide mouth and forced the corners bent-bow downward, but the deep-carved tension lines around his mouth-corners were so shaped as to reveal that he was hard-suppressing glee; his chest was tormented by the heavy breathing that flared his nostrils, a breathing required by the oxygen demands of his charging metabolism.

Why? Because . . .

As surely as the consequent of a validly premised-and-operated syllogism, the galactic system created by Croyd *was destroyed—already*! That was to say: Dino Trigg had constructed the mechanism for the specific and accurately aimed chain reaction, had arranged the ingredients, and—using the incomparable Zauberger musicianship, playing on Frey's expertise as Frey played on the ultrasynthesizer—Dino was about to pull the trigger.

And was it not just another instance of Dino-inspiration brought to fruition under pluperfect Trigg-control?

In his hyper-euphoria, Dino was ready to walk on his hands atop the wrought-collodion railing of his turret-balcony. He had set up a physical certainty; and in the logic of spacetime, wherein pasts and futures are relative, any eventuality that is absolutely certain has already happened. "Done! all but done! he caroled, loudly so that he could hear the enchantment of his own lyric tenor above the thunder of the far-below surf; even so, he had to listen in his head to hear his own voice because the gusting wind, which had finally kept him off the rail of his desire, blew away his voice before it could reach his ears. Nevertheless, his impromptu chant continued, grew louder, began to be accompanied (on the scant four square meters of this balcony) by the sort of Tellenic dance which begins more slowly than a pavane but gains in velocity and exuberance until it culminates in frenzy . . .

. . . But before the solitary Dino-dancing reached that height of final fever, it slowed—as he became aware that *another* occupied this balcony.

Stopping rigid, he turned to stare at—*his other self*, who sat cockily perched on that same slender rail with his feet resting on filigree and his hands folded between his wide-apart knees; who rocked back and forth irregularly, leaning back over ocean against a wind gust, straightening when it died.

His Darkside double said in Dino's mind: *Goodness gracious, friend Dino, I do believe I have caught you on the verge of waylaying Croyd and announcing your intentions!*

The notion of pre-announcing to Croyd was new to Dino, it had never occurred to him. Then if his doppelgänger was merely his own projection, how . . . But wait: perhaps Dino had entertained the idea subliminally, and his hintermind was using the projection of the golden god to make the idea explicit to his conscious apperception. Only, his double had seemed to put it to Dino as an idea that might not be very good; whereas Dino was finding it delicious, not that it was out in front of him teetering there on the rail.

Playfully Dino demanded: "Now Darkside, if I should so choose, which I don't, why should I not pre-announce to Croyd? My galactic jet-spume is a sure thing, logically an already-done thing; the Zauberger music is already in my sluiceways. Now I think about it, I could even compel Croyd to be the one who would *start* it—and Croyd would then enjoy the hyper-agony of watching all of it inexorably maturating by action of his own hand!"

But how in any universe could you compel him? Darkside demanded. *You've already blown your charisma for him; and don't suggest projective hypnosis, because you blew that even with board members, whereas Croyd is non-allergic to that. No, Dino, I have a better idea—will you listen to all of it?*

"Express it, and I will judge whether it is better."

Keep Croyd ignorant of your activities until you actually get your jet aimed and started—

"Profoundly I thank you; that is what I intended to do all the time."

You are fretfully prone to interrupt prematurely. That way lies chronic ignorance.

"I take your point; forgive me. Do complete your expression of your better idea."

Will do. Having got your jet actually started, moderate the acceleration that you had planned for it. Give it, say, two weeks to develop before it breaks into germinality and begins to envelop Sol Galaxy.

"Advantage?"

Having committed your jet to irresistible growth, notify Croyd—and enjoy his two weeks of frantic and unavailing efforts to stop it before it hits his galaxy.

Dino considered the proposal, while Croyd-projected Pseudo-Darkside, smiling friendlily, continued rocking on the rail. "And how," presently queried Dino, "do I notify Croyd?"

Grinning broadly, Darkside spread hands. *He will naturally be concentrating his attack on the hot-spot tip of the jet. You simply climb aboard the jet and ride it up to him. Fancy his amazement when you step triumphantly out of it!*

Now Dino stared, incredulous, at his golden likeness who had just delivered himself of an utter non sequitur. Was his projected image truly such a mental nothing? or was his mental image mocking him? In either case . . .

Abruptly Dino was soul-and-body fury-filled. "CLOWN!" he yelped; and striding to the rail, he swung on the gold-bearded jaw of Darkside, connecting explosively hard.

Pseudo-Darkside went spinning out into sky—and the spin slowed as the pseudo-body smallened, and presently the spin stopped, leaving a tiny upright incandescent floating Darkside grinning at his client

and vanishing.

At the same instant, Dino awoke to the agony in his knuckles, and looked at them, and saw that they were bleeding, and awoke dismayingly to comprehension that this Darkside had to be objectively real!

Soul-chilled Dino felt his energies oozing out of him; or perhaps his energies were contracting with the cold of his soul.

But Dino had recognized during many years that his personality was cycloid, alternating prolonged manic phases with perilous depressions. His major acquired self-discipline was to channel his manias into constructive hypo-euphoric moods, and to explode his depressions into compensatory hyper-mania which would gradually subside into upbeat normality. Now, on the high balcony, he reached deep into himself for the dynamite.

Successfully, it blew!

Thoroughly steamed up, he went into leonine balcony-pacing—which several times apotheosized itself into an actual hand-walking of the thin rail while carnivorous waves fifty meters below him slammed themselves white-foaming on rocks in feeding frenzy which upside-down he watched in crashing empathy:

Back to Hell with you, Darkside or Lucifer or whoever you are! I am a big shit, you are only a little shit! Your intricate Croyd-ploy was tempting indeed; it was precisely that, temptation, and extremely dangerous, it could have ruined everything, indeed the proposal to enter my created jet-spume and fly outward was sheer insanity, I mean yes I am sure that I could do it but I would not try, my own plan is most definitive, I do not propose to complicate it with aesthetic diversions, I will hew to the main line . . .

Let's get it going!

Howling "YO! YO! *YO!*" in wild climax, he rushed into his tower apartment, raised the *Sterbenräuber* and Flaherty on ivisiradio, issued orders to Kolly and to Flaherty, then ran downstairs and through corridors to the master bedroom on whose door he pounded. When Frey sleepily opened, Dino yelled at him:

"Now hear this! Roll out tomorrow morning at five—at FIVE, dja heah me? We lift off aboard Flaherty at seven for the *Sterbenräuber,* we'll bring along your musical flakes, we'll invade a kind of space that you never dreamed of, you'll be listening while I broadcast into that wonderful space all your masterly performances—*and you can watch the results in space!* THIS IS IT, Frey Zauberger—the culmination of all you've been working toward: ultimate celestial creativity! And when all that is done, up and out we'll fly for holiday among stars!"

Dino crashed the door shut in Frey's paralyzed face, backran corridors and stairs, reentered his tower suite, set beside his bed an unopened bottle of dirado for now and some restorative pills for tomorrow, tore off his clothes, leaped naked into bed, opened the bottle, drank off the dirado, set down the bottle, passed out with the lights on.

13. Great Communication

Via ivisiradio, almost instantaneously across 200,000 light-years:

"Tannen—"

"Cheers, Croyd. Where are you, there?"

"Inside the ship's computer, here. I'm dying to know what sort of image of me you're getting."

"A wire-worm tangle, of course. How's your control, in there?"

"Well, I can do *this*. And—were you watching my fiasco with Dino, when I played Darkside?"

"I thought it was a nice piece of work, my friend. Particularly that final system of illusions: hard physical jaw-impact, bogus Darkside-body receding into space, outside blood and inside pain on and in the Trigg-knuckles—"

"I thought I blew it."

"How?"

"I was being too damn subtle. I knew he wouldn't accept straightforward negative advice from Darkside—it would be too much of a flip-flop to be credible. So I tried the device of recommending that his vendetta be carried to a point of ultimate absurdity: actually riding the jet that he planned to create. Result: I got punched, and now I've lost him."

"You planted a seed, it may yet germinate. Stay with it."

"But will the seed fly—you should excuse that mix?"

"Not a mix; there are seeds that fly. But—yes, that is uncertain indeed, my friend: this I understand. So does most of our board. So do most of our ministers, including, thank God, Security. We are taking maximum physical precautions, inadequate as they may be. Astrofleet is deploying itself in three ranks across the Dorado longitudes—"

"Between 0500 and 0600 hours?" Croyd was naming celestial coordinates, not a time interval.

"A bit wider, in fact. But all the ray-screening that they can provide will not stop the hot-spot tip of a galactic jet-spume more than sixty thousand parsecs long punching in with the energy of a quarter-million stars. The ships can partially neutralize it, but that is a suicide mission, and the crews know it. We can't hit the jet while it's young and tender, because it will be growing in uptime which none of our ships other than your *Sterbenräuber* can penetrate—and Dino and Kolly still control the *Sterbenräuber*—or can *you* now counter-control it?"

"Not yet. And I'm not progressing fast enough."

"Well: by the time when the full-grown jet snarls into the present, it will already be big enough to engulf every ship in our fleet. By which time it won't matter whether we still have a fleet or not."

"A bit disturbing, Tannen, eh, what?"

"Aye. But I know you, Croyd: you have a ploy or two in mind."

"Perhaps. Value dubious. Purely from panic."

"Care to tell me?"

"Better not. You would disapprove, and my concentration can do without that."

"But can our mutual coordination do without that? Doesn't each of us need to know what the other is going to do?"

"I think not, in this case."

"Why not?"

"I have faith in you, Mister President. Do have faith in me, even when I depart from the book and improvise. And that is what you are going to have to do, because right now I don't have the foggiest what I *can* do."

"Always I have faith in you, Croyd, as you well know. But—shouldn't you maybe order Captain Kedrin to kill him?"

"Whatever else I may do, I won't do that. In the first place, I absolutely *have* to see whether he will go through with his plan. But even if he does, I shan't have him killed, it would be his easy way out. Did I say *out?* that reminds me: I have to go now. Croyd out."

CLIMAX FOR THE JET-MASTER

14. Detonation

Celestially entranced Frey and Freya, clutching hands together in paired chairs on the *Sterbenräuber* President's Bridge, peered into star-blurred space while the yacht plummeted two billion years into uptime; watched their Lesser Magellanic Cloud shrink and coalesce with its even smaller neighbor-cloud to form a single fishbowl-size galaxy with hazily shimmering mantle and fountains, while the Greater Magellanic Cloud shrank also to fishbowl size but remained separate at minuscule distance. The awed Hudibrasian bird-people observed the Flaherty-marshaled roboats maneuvering themselves into circular cyclotron-formation with respect to their yacht; the Zaubergers clung half-frightened as transcolor conferred upon them visual experience of Trigg-engendered energy-building radiation that whirled with ever-increasing intensity from boat to boat to ship to boat until its power was cosmic.

In semi-panic, the Zaubergers were closer together than ever they had been.

Dino and Kolly fed their guest couple at 1100 hours. By noon (ship's arbitrary time), Frey was back on the President's Bridge, accompanied only by Kolly—who could spare herself from the Operations Bridge which was pseudo-manned by command robots. Frey, and also Kolly to a lesser extent, braced selves for the start of the Frey-created supragalactic concert.

To Freya's distress, she had been excluded from the President's Bridge. Frey had said, not, "Dearest, I know you understand my need for solitude except for the necessary presence of Captain Kedrin," but instead, "Get that moron out of here!" And yet, together this morning they had been so *close* . . . Freya with a wounded shrug had accepted Dino's invitation to be with him, in the President's Living Suite which Dino had appropriated (with its holographic viewscreen-wall), while he in spectrally dimmed light played the ultra-stereophonic Zauberger flakes, therewith performing his deadly intergalactic surgery.

On the Dino/Freya viewscreen, as on the Frey/Kolly viewscreen, shone the paired galaxies: the re-coalesced Lesser Cloud (or rather, this cloud before part of it had split away) and the Greater Cloud beyond it; while a small, still-farther-off shimmering represented the Sol Galaxy containing Erth at a time when microscopic life was only beginning to evolve. All was in resolution so perfect that the nearest among these galaxies was not a fuzzy cloud but was instead a clustering of individual stars like the rosettes in a 150-screen color halftone under close scrutiny by perfect eyes. Not even static crackling penetrated from outside; not cosmic-ray sound-spattering, not the universally prevalent noise-residue coming in from the primeval Big Bang; the visuals brooded in the silence of eternity.

Now zhounded-in sound: big frightening sound, a system of polyphonic cadenzas, a demonic multi-plounding: they could see the three Magellanic galaxies blurring under the onslaught, for the intership cyclotron swelled the power of this output with all the radiance of several million stars. Only within their yacht, of course, could the term *sound* be applied to what they were experiencing; in space, it was rekamatic bombardment—which transformers in their observation equipment downgraded to visual range, so that it became a multicolor assault; the watchers could almost descry individual rays as they rained themselves into the galaxies, vanishing as they penetrated and maniacally energized atoms.

After hours of subtly changing musical bombast, its effect on the tiny galactic triplets was beginning to become visible. Red stars were going pink, pink ones were yellowing, yellows were going blue-white, blue-white ones virgin white. Now the galaxies had entirely blurred into multicolor clouds; and then

"HAUFENLAUGEN!" Frey rasped to Kolly by his side and through intercom to Dino and Freya. Each of the three galaxies had gone into color-mitosis! After a few minutes, during which all spectators held silent with eyeballs bulging, each galaxy had entirely twinned; and the new higher-frequency triplet was beginning to rise toward them leaving its lower-frequency mitotes behind.

Through intercom, Kolly told the Operations Bridge: "Hold spatial position for the moment, but adjust our downtiming speed so that we stay precisely this far ahead of those galactic mitotes; as of now, they are temporally gaining on us." (In the computer, the Croyd mindself had now achieved control over a multiple system of pertinent inhibitors; but for now, Croyd desisted, allowing the command robots to comply with Kolly's order.)

Terrified Freya quavered: "Please tell me what is happening."

To reassure her, tenderly Dino leaned toward her and slipped an arm around her torso between her upper and lower arms, explaining: "Your husband's music, elaborating my themes, has profoundly stung the souls of those three dead galaxies, resurrecting three newborn living galaxies out of them. The new galaxies are speeding in time toward their own future, developing far faster than their parents did, overtaking our present. Within days the new galaxies *would* burst into now—except that there is one more thing to be done with them first. Listen to the change in the music, and watch!"

Having been a many-valued cacaphonous fugue, the music resolved itself into a rhythmic soughing of thrust-and-draw, thrust-and-draw, sounding like *UGHhhh, HUHhhh, UGHhhh, HUHhhh*, endlessly, with every *UGHhhh* contorting their guts. Gradually it became apparent that the three new-budded galaxies WERE NEARER TOGETHER! and the *UGHhhh*'s emerging from the Greatest Cloud now began to be semi-answered by a series of depressedly ecstatic *HEHhhh, HEHhhh* sigh-groans from the masochized smaller galaxies. The mesmerized onlookers watched the two least clouds conjoin and coalesce into a single new-germinal Lesser Cloud; and now Lesser was being sucked into Greater— sucked *by* Greater whose gravitational intensity was being pulsatingly enhanced by the Zauberger *UGHhhh HUHhhh* noise-grindings.

"Now dammit, Trigg," fumed the voice of Zauberger, "you and I had agreed on a particular developmental order of these musical episodes to make a good overall composition, but you have viciously violated this order, and there will be critics who will guffaw and make mincemeat of these results—"

Dino suggested a thing to Kolly, who obliged with a split-screen effect that silenced Frey and was visible also to Freya. The left screen-half zoomed into the heart of the Greater Cloud, the right half into the center of the merged Lesser: the new-germinal clouds, not the old fossils. The watchers were primitively aroused by the intermix of supernova catastrophes intermingled with swirling black-hole hunger-darknesses in each of the two galactic nuclei; and always, the motion of the right-hand Lesser nucleus toward the left-hand Greater nucleus was perceptible . . .

Abolishing the screen-split, *Sterbenräuber* backed off a bit. Now the allured Lesser, all of it, was coming in upon the gravity-alluring Greater with the inevitability of a languid sperm drawn toward a gravid egg; the arousals of the spectators were almost sexual.

And then the galaxies were in contact.

And then . . .

Distressed Freya murmured: "Oh, my!" Leaning forward, biting all four thumbs, Frey grunted: *"Siegenliegen!"*

For the two galaxies had become one. Lesser was covered, or Lesser was devoured. Greater swelled. The video came in upon dinner-torpid Greater's nucleus: already black holes were beginning to multiply, and so was the population of supernovae, in this frighteningly accelerated burgeoning.

Overwhelmed by the unexpectedly cosmic power of his own music, Frey seized Kolly with his two right arms and hugged her to him. Kolly submitted as per Dino's instructions (and Croyd's reinforcement); and presently, still cold-submitting, she reflected that there were body-mysteries about these *Garbans* people—whereupon she moistened her lips with a hard-pointed tongue and submitted *softly*.

In the President's Suite, Dino was embracing Freya who had swooned against him; follow-up of *this* piquant trail was, however, for later. Just now he was mentally savoring his accomplishment of the most colossal legerdemain ever devised. It was done. The fossil galaxies *had* been made to spawn new buds of themselves; the newborn galaxies *had* merged, the amalgamation *was* fountaining vigorously, the fountaining *was* beginning to generate a central node of maximum energy which would surely become a jet—or, look: there already was the new jet's thin ghosting.

It had been accomplished without warning Croyd ahead of the actuality. It was now not merely a logically done thing, it was an *actually, kinetically* done thing!

Wearily, Dino Trigg concluded that there was no real need to tell Croyd what was about to happen to Croyd's galaxy. When the effects would start being apparent to Croyd, *that* would be when to explain. Darkside be damned!

15. Surprises in Bed

Early that morning, prior to the musical business of cosmic rearrangement, the Zaubergers had been ornately welcomed aboard the grinning yacht by Captain Kedrin accompanied by a small retinue of command and crew robots (among which, the former were androids). Valet robots had been assigned to the guests who in turn had been assigned to a three-room suite adjacent to the President's Suite; each of their bedrooms opened onto their central salon and also had doors offering immediate access to a corridor. Neunbals, which Dino had brought along, had been assigned to the kitchen to ensure that the two Hudibrasians would be fed opulently in terms of their native tastes.

After the musical jet-engendering, Frey and Freya excused themselves from their respective companions, from Kolly in Frey's case and from Dino in Freya's case, in order to repair to their suite and prepare themselves for dinner. In their suite, they said little to each other (except that Frey kept testily knocking Freya's choice of dress), but each was thinking profoundly. During that hour, in a Dino-Kolly session which had begun stormily and had gradually subsided into a relational oil slick, Dino had persuaded Kolly that the situation could be sehr amusante, and could grow mehr amusante, if Kolly would tickle her own fancy by getting to know Birdman Frey in ways that would have to be titillatingly perverse. Would Kolly have spat into Dino's eye had not computerized Croyd requested (i.e., commanded) that she go along? interested Kolly wasn't sure.

During hours in the stardomed lodge (real stars, but not clearly featuring Doradus because this was two billion years ago), the Zaubergers emitted ohs and ahs while replenishing their oh-ah energy with delicately blended wines given tang by an exotic assortment of small Hudibrasian undersea creatures immersible in a variety of piquant sauces. Thereafter, dinner was constituted by bewilderingly diversified dishes, inspired by Hudibras and by Erth, accompanied by more wines and seductive flakemusic.

Whereafter well-coached, not-unwilling Kolly found pretext to conduct Frey on a guided tour of the yacht. This freed Freya to move with Dino forward to the President's Bridge for an hour of pre-prehistoric star-study with the swiftly growing jet-spume front and center. (Part of Dino's musical jet-formation process had been to tilt the amalgamated galaxy so as to aim the jet precisely at Sol Galaxy.)

A time came when Dino pointed out to Freya that there would be greater comfort in his private salon which had an equally intriguing celestial view. At first, Freya timidly demurred; but when Dino finger-stroked Freya's back between the two pairs of shoulder-blades and queried what harm there could be in it, Freya yielded, although not without perturbation.

Affairs with Frey developed rather more readily than Kolly had anticipated: clearly, Cosmically Successful Performer Zauberger was hot, aggressively wanting Liebesmahl after his long period of self-driving under Dino's musical carrot-and-whip. It was not so very long before tall Frey was gently massaging one-hand the upper back of diminutive Kolly while, standing side-by-side at ease in Frey's boudoir, they studied stars, holding drinks in mutually leeward hands.

Encouraged by Kolly's acceptance of the high massage, Frey added a hand a bit lower; and Kolly, making a moue, tabled her drink. Increasingly titillated, Frey shelved his, took both of Kolly's hands in two of his own, engaged Kolly's eyes, used his free hands to finger-touch Kolly's chest while finger-touching also his own. Kolly, allowing her eyes to go dreamy, nodded just perceptibly and, drifting to the gravistat, turned gravity down to zero; whereafter she pushed off with her toes and drifted in semi-horizontal languor above Frey's bed before the ravenous eyes of Frey—who aggressively pursued the issue, until at white heat, floating all but naked above eiderdown-recumbent Kolly, deliciously Frey removed from Kolly the ultimate small garment

and paused

and stared down, while Kolly came alert to the shocked change in the Zauberger facial expression and the quivering distress of the Zauberger antennae.

Frey thrust *her*self (and *her* it was, in the semantics of Erth rather than the usages of Hudibras) up and away from Kolly so rapidly that her shoulder-blades gently kissed the cabin ceiling, while Kolly came up off her bed and stood naked upon it with her startled-inquiring face turned up to desperately confused Frey.

A possibility occurred to Kolly. She reached up, grasped the final small Zauberger garment, yanked it legward to bare what counted

and gaped at the

what, then gaped at the contorted Zauberger face

and clapped a hand over her mouth to hide a grin and stifle a laugh

and, after moments of struggle, achieved self-control, composed her face into tenderness, uncovered her mouth so that Frey could see its nevertheless-desire, and raised both arms high inviting Frey to come into her embrace.

For, later Kolly semi-reasoned within herself, *such misunderstandings are perfectly comprehensible when there are confusions of linguistics and usages as between alien cultures. For Hudibras, Dino and Frey are tall and dominant and therefore male, while Freya and I are small and yielding—at least, I yield to Dino, damn him—and therefore female. It just goes to show that the question, who is female and who is male, ends up as a matter of symbolic label-convention; and what really counts is, who has the babies. Well, all right: I undertook the duty of having perverse inter-species pleasure, and I got a surprising extra dimension of it; nobody loses, except . . .*

Hey: wonder how that sweet little Freya will react when that arrantly heterosexual sexist paranoid Dino discovers the truth . . .

Oho: more to the point—when Dino learns the truth and explodes, HOW will he explode?

While Kolly was tempting Frey, elsewhere the Dino-Freya romance was progressing like an intimate minuet. Freya continued deliciously timid in his presence; and because each Dino-touch caused small Frau Zauberger to shiver with some feeling or other while continuing to cling, Dino's passion exceeded anything he had known since the very first night with Kolly. They were midair-floating, Dino having considerately turned down the cabin gravistat—down, but not wholly off: a minim of gravity is piquant.

With climax near-distantly desirable, Freya uttered small: "o dino—o dino—dino, until now i have never been unfaithful to frey—" Caressing Freya, Lover Trigg low-hummed into Freya's ear: "Never think of this as infidelity; think of it as high romance." Instantly it quenched Freya's guilt: Frau Zauberger went all helpless, relaxing, enjoying

until deliciously Dino plucked away from Freya's loins the ultimate small garment

and paused

and stared down, while Freya came alert to the shocked change in the facial expression of militantly heterosexual mother-worshiper Dino Trigg.

Volcanic fury hot-flowed, engulfing the Trigg-brain, and his rigid right hand all the way up arm into shoulder and back swung in a hard arc backhand-smashing into Freya's head which cracked to its left, and he felt the crunch and heard-felt the neck snap, and Freya, surprised dead eyes wide open, was catapulted across cabin to bounce rubbery off a bulkhead while the Dino-body in reaction went into midair spin until with a small series of convulsive twists he stopped his own spinning and in profound reactive distress contemplated the now-purposeless drifting of the slaughtered Freya-body.

Twisting himself convulsively in midair, Dino swam to the gravistat and turned it up, dropping Freya heavily on the bed and himself upright on the cabin floor. He stared down at dead Freya whose groin displayed nothing at all that was anything but male in the semantic connotations of Erth or most planets that Dino knew about. Now it was ghastly apparent that Freya's equipment was female only in the semantics of Hudibras.

Dino in his machismo wore one small remaining garment which he had planned to shed for the final pounce. This garment had hard-bulged, but now it was contoured more serenely.

Dino said: "Scheiss." He buzzed out of the bedroom.

Myco! Croyd mind-hissed to the chief command-android. *Follow Trigg. I have to get started on this body—and then I can join you intermittently with Dino.*

Where frantic Dino wound up was on the exterior *Sterbenräuber* hull—dorsal, ventral, lateral, whatever: in uptime space it hardly mattered. He was now fully clothed, having distraughtly grabbed alternate clothing out of a dressing room in his suite. He hadn't bothered to suit up; nor was he magnetically shod, for the yacht maintained a system which would on command activate an external gravity field, and he had impulsively commanded it. He was pacing this hull swiftly, angrily, taking less than two minutes to slam feet along the three-hundred-meter lateral span of the hull-grin.

His fevered pacing didn't stop, it didn't stop, it kept going, once or twice he even ran a few paces, and the burden of his prancing was *godammit godammit I am mocked mocked* . . . Knowing that the viciously traumatic quality of this unintentional self-mockery had to be psychosexual, pacing he set himself the task of confronting the soul-reasons for it, even though the agony of this confrontation was far worse than the gut-contorting hell of squeezed balls.

(Croyd watched through the Myco-eyes, emphasized, began finally to form a plan . . .)

Well, yes (pacing): of course, being entirely heterosexual, Dino's discovery of Freya's unexpected maleness would have terminated his desire—but why, being an arcane cosmopolite, would the revelation have (pacing) driven his soul into a Freya-killing frenzy? why had this unveiling spewed into him a brutal sense of ultimate personal defeat after his monstrous triumph of galactic-jet generation?

Pacing, he glanced sidewise at his glowing, burgeoning jet for reassurance: it was growing as it downtimed toward germinality in its accelerated evolution, but the *Sterbenräuber* had been set to downtime at the same rate staying ahead of the jet, and Dino out here still was part of the yacht's inertial system; so his sense that the jet was relatively larger now, and angrier, was doubtless an illusion . . .

(Croyd, having dealt with the Freya-body, was computer-watching Dino. Croyd now understood what to do, and he prepared to do it. Dino in soul-crisis was ripe for decisive seduction by another Croyd-stimulated, Dino-projected Pseudo-Darkside who could now persuade Dino to seek out Croyd and recklessly challenge him with an abortive revelation . . .

Only, something else happened first, and the phenomenon was unsettling:

Dino paused in midstride, hit by something between a realization and a self-serving decision. He bellowed into silencing space where all primitively sonic vibrations, having made it through a larynx, are hushed at the lips: "DARKSIDE! *YOU* DID IT TO ME! GO BACK TO YOUR HELL, MY UNSAVORY DOUBLE! CROYD IS MY FIRST ENEMY, BUT BE ASSURED, YOU ARE MY SECOND! BY HELKENFLITZEN, MY SEDITIOUS DOUBLE, ONCE I WILL HAVE DONE WITH CROYD, I'LL BE DEALING WITH *YOU!*"

So did Dino, by cursing the devil, inadvertent-

ly align himself on the side of God
                              *only, the devil
responded!*
   Croyd was now astonished and aroused by *himself seeing* the golden double whose role he had
enacted and had been intending to reenact. He
had supposed that Darkside was Dino-imagined;
and on the Zauberger balcony, Croyd had successfully Dino-projected this god; but now, there *was*
Darkside, floating in uptime-space in front of Dino
and a bit above him; and the shocked posture of
Dino as he stared at his double confirmed that
Darkside was a shared phenomenon and therefore likely to be real.
   But the exchange between Dino and Darkside
astonished Croyd by its disappointing brevity!
   Said Dino eagerly, while his double regarded
him with every appearance of being crashingly
bored: "Hey, Darkside, *welcome* you are, my need
for you is enormous, you are indeed godly-
magnanimous to return after my ill-mannered
hastiness—"
   Lethargically responded Darkside: *I came only to
give you notice that I am bugging off. It was a good ride
for a while, Dino; but the good part has come to a close,
and ennui is beginning to threaten; and after all these
millennia, I know when to call quits to an adventure.
Toodle-oo!*
   Darkside vanished.

   The abandoning of Dino by his darkside-double,
just at this time of Dino's perverse triumph, simply *had* to precipitate a soul-crisis in Dino. The
urgency now for Croyd was to concentrate ship's
attention upon Dino while psychically he would be
dealing with this crisis: perhaps Croyd could use-
fully intervene with some gentle nudging, without
revealing himself.

I need to be aware, Croyd cautioned himself, *that if the jet catches up with us, it can destroy all life aboard Sterbenräuber*. But unless he could think of a way to eject Dino from the ship's inertial system, he saw no alternative.

"Correct me if I am wrong, Croyd. One: the jet will not destroy Dino's life, because of his defenses." It was the i-radio voice of Interplanetary Union President Tannen.

Unsurprised Croyd responded: "Not unless Dino should panic and fail to set up those defenses."

"On the other hand, if that should happen, we would have to accept the loss of Dino, because in fact he did go through with his villainy."

"True."

"If we do lose him, will you recover, Croyd?"

"All except a part of me, I guess. God damn it, he *has* to be possessed—"

"Compris; d'accord. But while you are doing whatever you may decide to do in the service of our galaxy, I dare hope you will remember that there are three jet-destructible human lives presently aboard your ship, the Zaubergers and Kolly."

Croyd retorted: "There is also the brain of *Sterbenräuber* for which I have come to feel a certain affection, being in it. Even the robots, like Myco and Flaherty, have some kind of humanoid value."

"Those lives, I agree, should not be tossed away cheaply. On the other hand, the stakes are not cheap."

"And on still another hand, Tannen, although the timing is frighteningly close, if we can just manage to—"

"Time it right, my very dear friend. Tannen out."

"Croyd out, —with affection and determination." Out.

*   *   *

Deliberately, then, Croyd committed himself to death-jeopardy by deactivating, in the ship's computer, certain among the inhibitor-fields that he had mastered: those which would enforce his prior command that the *Sterbenräuber* downtime toward the germinal present just fast enough to stay a fixed time interval ahead of the swiftly downtime-burgeoning jet-spume.

After that, Croyd was ready to redirect his attention into the multiclone lab of this endlessly clever yacht. There, what remained of Freya, whose return from death could be crucial for several galaxies, was now dormant but entirely reconstituted under robotic ministration.

Having caused Freya to be returned into the bed in the Presidential Suite which Dino had at least temporarily abandoned, Croyd brought Freya into gentle awakening and stayed in mental contact with Freya's mind. Freya's eyes came open, he sat up in bed; he looked around him for Dino his lover, recalling nothing of the murder-assault.

Said Croyd via intercom: "Dear Freya, forget him, he will not return, and I want to talk with you a little about that. My name is Croyd."

Freya stared at the intercom outlet. Freya ventured: "Not—*the* Croyd?"

"Aye."

"Oh, Mr. Chairman, I *so* admire you!"

"Thank you. That's nice. Now listen, Freya. I am going to lecture you briefly about the flip side of sexuality. After that, I am going to tell you a way for you to exploit the situation for your long-range good. Whereafter I suggest a cold shower followed by about an hour of time killing before you go to your quarters, confront your husband with Captain Kedrin, and try out my ploy."

16. Adversary vs. Adversary

Awakening in the Zauberger bed, nakedly supine Kolly (who, a while back, had taken advantage of a rest interlude to adjust gravity somewhat upward) turned her head to consider nakedly snoringly supine Frey Zauberger beside her. Again she experienced a stirring as she surveyed the several obvious anatomical differences in this Garbans female-termed-male. She lay indolent, viewing and reviewing possibilities . . .

She became intuitively aware that they were not alone. Turning her head away from Frey, she saw a fully clothed Freya Zauberger who had penetrated into the bedroom and stood hesitant near the door which he had closed behind him.

Queried Kolly presently: "Would you prefer that I leave you alone with Frey?"

Freya decisively head-negated.

Kolly, repressing a yawn, decided that the situation was interesting. She asked: "Will you awaken Frey—or shall I?"

Freya uttered: "You."

Sitting up, Kolly tapped a Zauberger upper shoulder; sitting up, Frey swung startled to Kolly, then gaped at Freya beyond. Kolly having punched her pillow into suitable contours, reclined to enjoy the action.

Characteristically, Frey went aggressive-cruel. "Ah

there, Dummy. What are you—some kind of voyeur?"

Uncharacteristically, Freya counterattacked, brows frown-down (and Freya's down-brows were forty-centimeter antennae.) "Caught in fragrante relicto, hey, my husband? I've managed to accept a whole marriage-full of your nasty domineering macho, but this is a bit much, don't you think?" Anger-trembling, Freya awaited Frey's reply, waited in gently weaving enemy-readiness that was wholly new in Frey's experience of Freya.

Frey snarled: "Will you kindly tell me what I have done with Kolly that you have not done with Dino?"

Shoulders back, unmammae'd pigeon-breast out, Freya answered in a dead smoothness of fury: "With Kolly, clearly you have done a great deal. With Dino, I have done *nothing! nothing at all*, dammit! All right, husband, I will give you the benefit of all the doubt that I can possibly whomp up, I will accept that this was a one-night seduction by a lecherous tempter at a time when you were taut and fatigued and frazzled and needed sinful novelty. But I too was tempted, by Dino, and I did not fall; and the contrast between us has finally straightened out my focus on this marriage. You are *not* superior to me! You are *NOT* superior to me, except in your scheissty musicianship; in every interpersonal and judgmental way, you are dammit *inferior* to me! And if you ever so much as *hint* at putting me down, I swear I will cut off your antennae and stuff them side-by-side up your wavular cloaca!"

As Frey's lower jaw slowly sagged open, Freya's attention turned to the naked Kedrin genitalia; and Freya said disconcertingly to Kolly: "Say, now, you Erth-males *are* different from us, aren't you!"

Kolly came out of bed and began rerobing herself, all the time watching the two principals in this amazing marital combat and expecting a Frey-explosion. But a distraction arrested her with her pants half on. The intercom baritone-lilted: "Captain Kedrin, tell the Zaubergers how your mutual charm-god Dino is using them. That is an order. Over."

Swinging to the intercom, hard-smiling down-browed Kolly responded: "Order heard and accepted, Mr. Chairman. It's a pleasure!" Then she told stonefrozen Frey: "Your music has triggered a process that will destroy your galaxy. Your Vanador is already doomed—and so are you, and so is your Freya—by what Dino Trigg has made you play on your diabolical ultrasynthesizer!"

Frey, having stared, breathed: "Is my castle safe?"

Having appraised the idiocy of his mate, Freya tuned on Kolly and flared: "Forget my husband, deal with me. Why are we being destroyed, and what can we do about it?"

Kolly precised: "Your husband or wife, whatever, produced music that ended by generating a new combined Magellanic Galaxy and driving it into accelerated evolution. When the new galaxy emerges into germinality, which will be awful damn soon, it will destroy both preexisting Magellanic Clouds because there will be room in that space only for the new one; and the Zaubergers and all their Hudibrasian friends will be dead because it will turn out that your Hudibras never existed."

Freya gaped. Dead-eyed Frey demanded: "*My* music will do *that?*"

"*Has* done it, you stupid mark, *has* done it! So whaddaya think, Zauberger: wanna stop the process?"

Freya blurted: "Yes we do!" Semi-paralyzed Frey contemplated her mate-liberate.

Kolly turned to the intercom: "Chairman Croyd, pray favor us with your thought."

Croyd told them: "This is not a certainty, but I think the new-germinal activity *might* be erased if you could find the music flakes—"

"Well?"

"And replay them. But backward. And I mean, completely in reverse from precisely the order in which Dino just played them."

Frowning her mighty antennae, Frey murmured: "Yes, of course, we should do it, we *must* do it, we *will* do it. Only—"

"Good, GOO-ood!" purred Croyd. "So where are the flakes?"

Frey vibrated her beakflab over it. She said then: "Trigg told me that he was keeping the tapes in his private safe. But where *that* might be—"

Freya announced: "I know where the safe is! After he left me because he was frustrated by my perfect fidelity to this dummox Frey, I explored the suite, and—"

Croyd commanded: "Lead on!" And bemused Frey found herself rearward in a procession resolutely led by Freya behind whom prowled Kolly.

In the Trigg-suite, they gathered in front of the safe which Freya had revealed by swinging back a side-hinged painting. There was, however, no visible combination lock. How to attack it?

Calling the bridge, Kolly summoned her prime command robot Myco which (released now from its Croyd-behest to watch Dino) joined the group in the Trigg-suite and studied the safe. "Minister Trigg," it told them, "did make me privy to the nature of the key, it was merely his palm-pressure; but because I am physically so different from him—"

Yelled Frey: "TRY, for the love of Schnarliwarli!"

The galvanized android placed its four-fingered

right palm against the sensor. There was a click, and the safe-door small-jumped ajar. Kolly leaped at the safe, shouldering the android aside. Out of the safe, Kolly hand-raked all that was in it.

No music flakes.

Doom for Hudibras. And for Erth. And for both Magellanic Clouds. And for Sol Galaxy.

Stunned by the terminal exodus of his resident god whose immanence had for so long passion-powered him and in whose existence he had come to believe, Dino dull-stood wherever he was standing and gazed at the glowing phallos that he had created, the galactic jet-spume which was meant to bring about the deaths of three galaxies: Lesser Magellanic, Least Magellanic, and Sol-cum-Croyd. And after a while, he began to notice that the burgeoning venom of that cosmic sting was not arousing him at all, at all.

Instead, the abrupt loss of his powering Darkside was troubling him in ways which he would not have anticipated. Struggling to formulate the complexity of his disturbance, he hit upon the idea of striving for understanding through an orderly review of what Darkside's advent had meant for him. During all his career life, until Darkside, Dino had been pathetically earnest in his devotion to duty and control, and the rare times when Croyd had drawn him into dancing fun had invariably been followed by annoyance at himself; whereas Darkside had released him into a new career of exalted joy. When Dino's Darkside-aroused ambition had been malevolently defeated by that same Croyd whom Dino had loved and served, Darkside had been faithful; had rescued him from suicide; had made himself known to Dino, had midwived Dino through a swift self-analysis culminating in understanding of the self-serving Croyd-villainy which had secretly underlain his patron's fostering devotion; had enabled Dino to spread for himself a revenge-design whose epochal splendor reduced the legend of Lucifer's malevolence to farce level.

And just when Dino's clever and laborious fiend-construct had been activated in glory—*that* snarling glory, right out *there* . . .

He then discovered that he was standing spread-legged on the ship's belly. Aaa, nah! Angry at himself for sliding into this ridiculous stance, he scrambled around a flank until he was fully dorsal again, just aft of the central nose-grin. Reenergized by his contempt for fugitive Darkside, here he took a new spraddling stand, arms wide, fists clenched, head backtilted, hair streaming backward in nonwind, face toward stars—toward remote galaxies including the fuzzy little spiral called Sol Galaxy which was his home and his target.

Aloud into sound-smothering uptime void he yelled: "I can do without your piddling help, my gone Double! You simple silly, running away from the human engenderer of a galactic metageyser merely because I frustrated your childish urge to be in me experiencing perverse dalliance with a male bird! And you are noticing, I hope, that I brought off my jet—*my* jet, Darkside, and ours no longer—without help from Croyd: it was begotten immaculately by Dino Trigg upon three galaxies!"

He halted, mind brushed by a piquancy. Now, there was absolutely no reason why he shouldn't, and every reason why he should, seize upon Croyd and gleefully tell him about impending ruination.

The notion should have given him joy. Why wasn't it giving him joy? Probably he was upset by the loss of divine afflatus; possibly also, Croyd having been a father-figure, there was a sense of sin. Good Crest! Dino could expunge *that* from himself as a trade off for the delight of the confrontation.

HE WOULD DO IT!

Wait, now: was there any way at all in which a warned Croyd could reverse the astronomical process which Dino had started and established so that already the death-jet was a thousand light-years long and sizzling outward almost at i-ray velocity? Let's be careful now.

There couldn't be any . . .

Oh yes there could! Let's by all means squelch that possibility before we attack!

Darting back into ship's interior, Dino hastened to the President's Suite. No sign of Freya in the salon; possibly he (aye, *he*) was weeping in the master bedroom. Dino opened the private safe, withdrew the canisters of flakes bearing the recordings of the Zauberger music, fed all the tapes into his nuclear garbage-disposal, once again leaped outside.

All space was now illuminated by his jet-spume. He must give it a name. *Deathfire?* no; corny. *War-Dog?* no. *Helljet?* nah . . .

An inspired whimsy hit him; and his grin was twisted, for the whimsy had been twistedly begotten upon him by his female music-master Frey Zauberger. Call the jet *Schnarliwarli!*

Spread-legged on the back of the grinning star rover, shock-paralyzed Dino Trigg taut-stared at the cosmic monster whose borning he had engendered and whose galloping growth now increasing threatened himself. The growth of his jet-spume was of course four-dimensional, but it described in spacetime a geodesic describable by two vectors: rate of growth in length, and rate of time-approach to the surface of actuality. The stem-length was now expanding at the rate of four hundred light-years per hour, and the rate was doubling hourly; already the undulating, incandescent stalk was more than 600 light-years long, and proportionally thickening, tipped by a hot-angry glans the size of a star-cluster.

Meanwhile, gradually it came through to jeopardized Dino, something had happened to halt the commensurate uptiming of the *Sterbenräuber*—which now was glued herewhen in temporal stasis, exposing himself *and Dino* to brain-and-body-riddling ionic engulfment. Minutes ago, the entire length of the jet from origin-galaxy to hot-spot tip had crossed perhaps a third of his visual field, with its linear direction relative to himself vertically upward (toward the whither that Sol Galaxy occupied). Now already he could not see both tip and base in a single glance; instead, he had to shift his gaze alternately upward and downward to encompass both; while the breadth of the uprushing stem, from having been laser-thin, was a quarter of his visual field thick, and thickening as it gained on him.

Staring horrified, he was at first indecisive about what to do. Go see Kolly? kick her into action? but his orders to her had been clear, so either she was deliberately negating, or she had lost control; so forget it. Abandon ship? downtime individually in the body? no way: he as an individual did not have the uptiming-downtiming *speed* of the yacht; him as an individual the jet would quickly overtake. Summon Flaherty? but Flaherty had been dispatched on other duty.

The stem-width was half his visual field and thickening; now, both mantle-origin and hotspot-tip were beyond the range of his vision when he stared as he was staring hypnotized at the stem.

As a final self-rescuing resort, he had always the option of killing his jet-creation—which he wouldn't think of doing, of course, being willing to sacrifice himself to his Croyd-vendetta—and yet it is intelligent to know your options even if you won't use them, so that was an option . . .

O God no it was *not* an option, because the only way to kill his jet involved the Zauberger music-flakes *which he had just vaporized!*

So here he stood, spread-legged on the back of his own gigantic grin, about to become not merely the cause but also *part* of galactic destruction.

In the face of certain death, some flee (but he could not), some shrivel (but he *would* not), some stand and defy. Dino turned-on a *Sterbenräuber*-grin energized by his own self-mockery; and he screamed at his jet—screamed silently into space, of course, but all his head vibrated as what would ordinarily activate waves of sound spewed out of his joyous jaws:

"Hey, Jet! You Jet! I aimed you at Sol Galaxy, remember! I aimed you at Croyd! I did something wrong, and now you are chasing *me*, but recall your orders: your target is Sol! And just in case you think you are shaking off your master by devouring me, forget it, because I'm joining you! *Joining* you, dja hyah me? So go, so roar: you can't escape my orders because I will be *part of you*, your guide, your death-god! And what will you do to me? Incinerate me? hardly, until you spew me all the way up to your hot spot. Ionically addle my brain-rekamatics? but I think I have defenses against that. Flatten me with thrust against inertia? anyone else, yes, in a hurry, but *not me*, Jet!"

The stem of plasma uprushing at many times light-speed now entirely filled his visual and mental world.

Kicking himself off the body of *Sterbenräuber*, he drove himself at his jet, exultantly screaming: "LOOK OUT, SPOUT! HERE I COME! WELCOME ME ABOARD!"

REALITY-FACING

17. Aboard Schnarliwarli

Terrifying turbulence whipped him like a terrier-whipped microscopic snake, and kept on whipping him prolongedly until his mind was flung free of his ion-addled bodybrain and he perceived that the body being whipped was his own—and that, apart from the rekamatic brain/body addling, there was an increasingly colossal inertial wind which grew with the growth of the jet aiming toward maturation at a length of two hundred thousand light-years beginning at zero in the timespace of thirteen hours from activation: a permanently brain-pulping nonshielded thrust which Dino's powers allowed him partially to counteract but not enough so for the preservation of sanity

          he sought to work his way back to himself, but his body kept vanishing and reappearing with face contorted in its grim unsouled brain-effort to cope when ionic intra-bombardment scrambled any possibility of coping which the brain might otherwise

          by now the face was a ghastly-distorted strontilite mask, and the brain was a shambles, and the mind out here separate from the body was almost equally addled by reason of its tenuous connection-filaments with its disintegrating mother-brain

          hours and hours while

his jet-spewn body kept vanishing and reappear-
ing and vanishing

Croyd reactivated the inhibitors, restoring the
automatic temporal interval which the yacht had
been ordered to preserve between itself and the
jet; only, the interval now was only a quarter what
it had been, so the yacht-cybernetics labored to
drive the yacht downtime at a compensating
acceleration.

Croyd whished; it had been a very near thing.

Through intercom, he called: "Now hear this,
Captain Kedrin! You and the Zaubergers get down
to the ultrasynthesizer console room and do what
you have to do! Croyd out!"

Internalizing his computer-vision, he watched
Kolly and the Zaubergers obeying his command.
Whereafter he gave all his attention to the remarkable spectacle of a literally electrified Dino
Trigg riding the swift expansion of the galactic
jet-spume which Trigg had created to spite Croyd
his benefactor.

Did the Zaubergers appreciate how tight the
time was, to bring off what Frey now had to bring
off in order to prevent the permanent mind-
scrambling of humanity and all animals throughout Sol Galaxy—while, at the same time, saving
their own galaxy and therefore their own planet
Hudibras—and therefore, of course, Frey Zauberger's ultimate joy, her Dino-given high house?

Standing by the ultrasynthesizer:
Frey: "It's a ridiculous assignment, I can't do it."
Freya, stern: "But you must!"
Frey, distraught: "But I *can't*—"
Reaching upward with her two top hands, grim
Freya let Frey have an open-palmed one-two on
the sides of Frey's face while Freya's two lower

hands firmed on Frey's torso to hold her for the punishment. Frey's eyes squeezed shut against the slapping, then opened to stare stonily at her new-aggressive consort. She began with frosted voice: "You didn't have to—"

"But I *did!*" yelled little Freya, wide-waving his upper hands while continuing to clasp tall Frey with his lower ones. "Good God, husband, I don't know what's been *subtracted* from you! don't you comprehend the incredible *brain* that you have? Would that brain find it insuperably difficult to replay all your music exactly as it was broadcast the first time? Well now, look: all you are being asked to do is—play it all in reverse, note-for-note *backward!*"

Trembling, Frey mounted the bench before the ultrasynthesizer. She poised hands, feet, antennae. Shivering took possession of her long body. She quavered: "But he played my music in a different order—"

Freya's reply was firmly bracing. "Now listen, my dear husband. You have your weaknesses in other respects; but musically, there is nothing you cannot do, and you know it, and *I* know it! Frey: so he played your music in a different order—so *recall* that different order, and play *that* backward!"

Intently at work within the computer, Croyd (wondering why the nonpareil computer of this wonderful ship hadn't automatically backup-recorded for ship's log the Zauberger music whether or not Kolly or Dino had wanted that) brought off an intricate system of astrogational adjustments. These ended by positioning the yacht at a particular vantage point of frozen motion with respect to the spatiotemporal geodesic being described by the generating-downtiming jet.

Disenfranchised and helpless Kolly, gazing at

the cycloramic video on the President's Bridge, stared at the resulting effects. The whole jet from galactic base to hot-spot tip was now vertical in the picture-frame. Its downtiming toward germinal present, with consequent growth, was known to be happening but was invisible. Generative extensional growth of the vertical jet also was known to be happening but was invisible, although the jet did waver and seem to be alternately stretching and contracting as the automatic ivideo-adjustments from instant to instant spotted changes a bit inaccurately and then self-readjusted.

The Croyd-mind of the computer was enriching Kolly's viewscreen with a small superimposed inset. In a flame-yellow circle near the base of the jet, but infinitesimally rising along the stem toward the tip, writhed a vastly magnified image of Dino Trigg. This close-up image was relatively enlarged so that his size appeared to be a quarter of the jet-stem thickness, although in fact Dino was no more than an infinitesimal of the jet's thickness and continually shrinking relative to its growth. He kept twisting within the jet-stem; and when occasionally he turned up full-face toward the *Sterbenräuber* (sometimes upside-down), his expression was horrid, as though he were gorgon-gazing.

Catatonically fascinated Kolly stayed in deep-freeze for an incalculable period of time, while the circle containing Dino appeared (in this perspective) to ooze upward along the jet-stem. The computer was now providing informational side-lettering:

| Growth Rate | | | | |
H-Hour Plus	Light Yrs per Hour	Length in Light Yrs	Distance from Sol in Light Yrs	Years Before Actuality
5	400	600	169,400	−1,200,000,000
6	800	1,400	168,600	− 980,000,000
7	1,600	3,000	167,800	− 810,000,000
8	3,200	6,200	163,800	− 640,000,000

Kolly, consulting the figures, grimaced and snorted: "Damn computer has no morals—" A percept brought her up short: Captain Kedrin, necessarily a mathematician, had noticed the numerical relationships: every hour, the *rate* of the jet's growth was doubling, while its descent from the deep past into germinal actuality was proceeding at a remorseless 170 million years per hour. These extrapolations meant that the jet formed profoundly in the past would break out into present actuality *only four hours from now*—which would give it time to overcome the jetless reality of the Magellanic Clouds and envelop Sol Galaxy only two hours later!

The ghastly concept, coupled with the hypnotic tri-d depth of the video, drew the conscious Kolly-self entirely out of the ship. She was in effect floating free in spacetime, seeing Dino directly without screen-mediation, as Trigg ascended along the jet-stem, while some demon provided glowing explanatory words over to one side. There were mesmeric periods when she seemed to be looking at some supernatural Dino-spirit who had catapulted himself radially upward from the surface of some planet at escape velocity toward a nonexistent moon . . .

A bluish-white glow was beginning to intrude from frame-top precisely above the hot-spot jet-tip yet still somewhat remotely beyond that tip. Kolly knew that the new shape was another galaxy: it was, in fact, her own Sol Galaxy. A shivering beset her: the galaxy was the jet's target, and in it, her planet Erth. Dino-Shiva, brazenly riding the stem of the jet that he had created with the aid of Kolly-Kali, goddess of fertility and of death (Kedrin was no illiterate), was about to realize his saturnine purpose whose full import Kolly, in her damnable infatuation, had never really grasped until now.

The video-encircled Dino-image was three-quarters of the way up the stem toward the hot-spot tip. The legend read:

H-Hour Plus	Growth Rate Light Yrs per Hour	Length in Light Yrs	Distance from Sol in Light Yrs	Years Before Actuality
10	12,800	25,400	132,400	−300,000,000
11	25,600	51,000	106,400	−130,000,000

The schedule remained implacable: in one more hour, the jet would actualize itself; in still another hour—curtains for Sol . . .

But, wait. Wasn't the galaxy-searing hot-spot tip, roiling with the energy of half a million suns, intended to disrupt all energy including mental energy in the target galaxy? Then should not his inhuman ride along the jet-stem have disrupted and therefore destroyed the Dino-mind so that he would be unable to appreciate his own triumph? Might he not even be dead? for his dreadful stonied expression was not changing.

Kolly's own mind, in the course of her prolonged concentration, was going abstract. The vertical jet became for her a dotted line extending itself beneath Dino as though it were representing and pseudo-animating the course of his self-lofting

into space; and the abstract circle that was driving
itself toward the dotted line's forward-upward tip
was the rising Dino, a projectile aimed at a concen-
trically circled target called Sol Galaxy

only, from
out of nowhere another swift dotted line headed by
a personalized circle whizzed horizontally across the
picture from right to center and coalesced with the
Dino-circle. The joined circles shimmered

and vanished.

Kolly was on her feet, distraught. With an enormous mental-moral effort, she collected herself and
stared at the picture which still contained the extending jet with its source the amalgamated Magellanic Cloud and its target Sol Galaxy—

but which did
not any longer contain any circle or any circle-
embraced Dino Trigg.

Remembering that she was the ship's captain,
she taut-spoke to the intercom: "Computer, give
me a replay of that—slow-mo, magnification max,
image divided into four quadrants. Execute!"

Now the lower left quadrant of the screen was
filled by Dino: the comet-god Asterios rising
through space, his divine golden hair streaming
out behind him (illusion, probably, since his hair
was neatly barber-tailored), his godface

fearsomely distorted.

As the comet-god began to ascent into the upper-
left quadrant, across the upper-right quadrant came
out of nowhere Triggward-plunging flame-topped
Croyd.

Croyd grappled with Dino.

They vanished.

Kolly caused ivideo to close on the point of
Croyd's first appearance. There was no source;
Croyd merely appeared.

(Natch. He had hit that spacetime-entry out of nontime—concerning which, Kolly had no knowledge.)

Croyd's voice filled the President's Bridge: "Captain Kedrin, are you there?"

Confused Kolly got herself into line and snapped: "Aye aye, sir."

"Kolly, you have the con, I have departed the ship. Now listen. You are to continue cruising in this spacetime-frame until Professor Zauberger completes her musical assignment successfully. If she fails, you will require her to try it again. You will continue this program until you are redirected by myself. If I never redirect you, then you will forever continue this program. Understood?"

Straightening, Kolly emitted a show of defiance. "Now why would you do such a thing as leaving me forever in this Tantalus bit?"

"Because, you poor fool—and you aren't normally a fool, but right now you are *being* a fool—because if Zauberger fails, everybody in Sol Galaxy including myself will be permanently mindless, and the Magellanic Clouds as you have known them will no longer exist. Where then will *you* be?"

Having gulped, Kolly responded small: "Point well taken. However—is there some way for me to know when I can quit the bit?"

"There is; but you have the con, and it will be up to you to discover how to know; and if you make a mistake and do the wrong thing, you will answer to me and to Astrofleet Command—if we then still exist. Okay, no more pish-tush. Croyd out."

18. Consequence of Backwards Music

When Dino drifted back into a sort of consciousness that was intelligently perceptive but unable to exercise will, he was floating in what he recognized as nontime. But some compulsion prevented him from inspecting the nonscene; instead, his eyes were immovably fixed on spatiotemporal reality—on his jet Schnarliwarli.

Lethargic Dino gazed, drifting. Listlessly he recognized that his jet was reaching nearly its desiderated length of 200,000 light-years, was only a few centuries short of the germinality which would make it all-of-a-sudden real. It was a mighty tree of incandescent polychrome flaring at the tip into hot-spot foliage which was about to envelop Sol Galaxy.

One who appeared to be Darkside, glow-floating a little way off, wore an expression that seemed faintly melancholy as he spoke in Dino's mind: *So here you float, acknowledging your own helplessness.*

Dino chose to answer aloud in silent nonspace: "I? Helpless? In view of this colossal destruction that I have created? Oh, come, now!"

Helpless, aye: hung here in nontime by this arch-villain Croyd, hung in perfect position for watching the destruction of his galaxy. So helpless that even if you wanted to stop this destruction, you would be powerless to do it. I mention the paradox only because you felt strong enough to taunt Croyd by revealing to him your truly admirable villainy—and to do so against my advice, which doubled the audacity of the act. Clearly it had not crossed your mind that by douching him with the fire-venom of your hatred, you might thrust him beyond vengeance by fatally breaking his heart. But at least, Dino, it proves that you are purely malevolent, you even goose yourself.

Angered: "Go ahead, sandpaper my balls!"

Sorry. I'm not really sorry, but it's a nice thing to say. The big thing is, I am delighted that you are holding to your destruction of Sol Galaxy. Even if you should now change your mind and try to stop the process that you have started, you could not do so. In my view, this makes your decision so pure that it can be called holy. You have contemplated the robust power-future that would have been yours if, instead of destroying the galaxy, you had decided merely to kill Croyd and to substitute yourself into the resulting power-vacuum. That would have been the materialistic yuppy-choice. But instead, in your ethereal sainthood, you have elected for no future at all.

Cosmic silence.

Quietly said Dino, having licked lips: "I do not want Sol Galaxy destroyed."

You don't? Why? Because you love its people?

"Come off it, Darkside: I have never loved people."

Because you love Croyd, then?

"Ha!" But Dino found the question disconcerting.

Because you love to be powerful—and to be admired?

"Well—"

Power you have demonstrated: power at a godly level, power challenging anything ever attributed to Yah of the Sinites. You have merged a trio of galaxies into one, you have raised up a galactic jet-spume, you have acceler-ated two billion years of galactic evolution into the space of hours, you are about to destroy all society and there-fore virtually all human life in still a fourth galaxy. As for admiration, I admire your achievements, even though I have escaped from your now-boring person.

After heavy silence: "Four difficulties, Darkside. One: the achievements of that sort of power invariably turn out to be self-terminating. Two: *your* admiration I can do without, and I won't be finding any other admirers. Three: as for destroying in order to created, I haven't been able to think up any galactic social system that I might create which would improve on Croyd's destroyed one in terms of actualities and envisioned potentials. Finally, as to this marvelous new jet that I have created, my achievement lacks one desideratum: reversibility. I cannot destroy it."

Do you want to destroy it?

Dino coughed; whereafter he emended: "I meant to say that I could not destroy it even if I wanted to."

Are you sure you could not?

"Well, of course, if you should care to help me—

NO, STOP! DON'T HELP ME EVER AGAIN! I *have* it, Darkside: this is purely hypothetical, you understand, because I wouldn't think of activating the whimsy; but recall that I generated the jet with *flakes* of Zauberger music, and I could—"

Play the flakes in reverse?

Subdued: "I destroyed the flakes."

But surely the magnificent Dino Trigg could himself play all the cadenzas backward from memory?

Dino raised his chin. "No, I could not. But what does it matter, as long as this is purely hypothetical?"

It matters because it establishes how purely you are specialized as a destroyer par excellence. Your miserable creativities, even, have been instrumental to destructive purposes. Now it appears that you have moved on over

*the brink: you cannot destroy your own creation because
you destroyed the means of destruction. Having been
taunted with that unpleasant irony, will you now follow
your frequent bent by lapsing into psychotic depression?
Be warned that I will not again boost you out of it!*

Darkside hung there, coppery now and dull-
incandescent, in front of nonspace-hanging Dino—
who did indeed feel depression beginning to creep
into him. Darkside, his doppelgänger, wore a
crooked smile, and his arms were folded signify-
ing decision.

Resolutely Dino thrust away depression; up came
his chin, and he stood at graceful ease in his
floating, with his left arm and leg slightly advanced and his hair irrationally blown by nonwind.
"I have never felt depression," he asserted, "except when you have been in me."

*Come now: after you were defeated by Croyd and
space-hung in a decaying Neptune-orbit, was it not I
who pulled you out of a death-depression?*

Dino, resolute: "I would never have defied Croyd
unless you had been in me exciting me into it. I
now think that my depression after my defeat was
your depression after your defeat. I think that
you are a mood-god who falls into his own depressions and rebounds out of them into irrational
highs and imbues his host with his own moods of
extremism. And as to the question of my ability to
destroy my own jet, it is you who must taunt
yourself; because I have only to find Herr Frey
Zauberger, who is likely in fact to be Frau Zauberger
now I think about it, and I can require him, or
her, to play all her music backward from *her* unbe-
lievable musical memory. You doubt that she can?
I have endless confidence in her, I *know* that she
can."

Darkside challenged: *Prove it.*

"You will have to take it on faith; because, as I

keep reiterating, this is all hypothetical, and I do not really want to do it."

In that event, my former friend, I can only express my heartfelt sympathy, because it does appear that the destruction of your destructivity is already in progress. LOOK AT YOUR JET!

The transcoloration of the jet was dimming, the image was going all pointilla, the points were losing concrescence . . .

The jet was gone. And far below, the same sort of degeneration was invading Dino's consolidated Magellanic Cloud.

Dino collapsed upon himself—not in depression, but in the sort of twisted emotional relief that a compulsive and sin-conscious flagellant might feel if a force beyond his control should take his whip away.

Tannen told Croyd: "In subconscious fact, this is the way he really wanted it."

Frey Zauberger aboard *Sterbenräuber* brought off the backwards last of her dino cadenza-variations, leaned back on the bench of her ultrasynthesizer, closed eyes, lapsed into trance. They let her alone.

After a while she opened eyes, felt a face close to hers, turned her head a little, recognized that the head was Freya's: behind Frey's music-bench, Freya had hung his chin on her shoulder.

Frey dull-queried: "Did it work?"

"We have confirmation that it did. How could you doubt that it would?"

Frey down-frowned, thinking. Presently she closed eyes and ventured: "How could you hold such faith in me, after all these years of me kicking your teeth in?"

"Maybe," Freya suggested, "you kicked faith into me."

"I cannot guarantee that it will never happen again."

"Thank you for honesty, finally. Let me give you a counterhonesty: I would have surrendered to Dino, only she got hung up when she found out that both of us were female. All right, that's done. I'm having Captain Kedrin deliver us immediately to Hudibras, we have this old castle of ours to go over for repair needs; there are instances of dry rot."

The heavy Tannen voice now came into Dino: "I think the adventure is all done, Croyd. The jet and the new galaxy have dissolved back into the undifferentiated cosmos, and the two Magellanic Clouds are as they were, the Zaubergers are now the good opposite of the crumbiness that they were because of Frey's arrogant macho. I don't yet know whether we can forget Kolly Kedrin, but she will have to face you and me before we decide whether to remand her for court martial.

"Now, dear friend Croyd, what seems to remain is, the judging of Dino Trigg."

"Agreed," responded a familiar and love-hated baritone. "Do you agree that we should now proceed with the necessary confrontations?"

"I do. I suggest that you be the first to confront him."

Floating Dino felt himself growing gravity-loaded; and presently he foot-plopped

onto the golden-filamental breezeway-bridge between the two white towers of Croyd's nontime house. He was almost eyeball-to-eyeball with Croyd.

19. Showdown

Dino and Croyd stood facing each other on the bridge; they were some ten paces apart. Both men were wary.

Tannen invisibly hovered. The interplanetary president was barely controlling taut anxiety, mainly for Croyd, importantly also for Dino whom he liked and Croyd son-loved.

Dino, completely alert, demanded: "What?"

Croyd silently pointed at a revolver which lay at their feet about halfway between them. It was a museum piece: a post-medieval, early twentieth-century Colt forty-five.

Dr. Trigg, a part-time amateur of antiquities, twisted his mouth in a scornful grin. "High noon, Master? We wrestle, and one of us gets the gun?"

"Good thought," said Croyd, "but no. *You* pick it up."

After hesitation: "Why not?" Dino possessed the gun, stepped back, examined it, broke it to make sure that it was fully loaded, shook all six cartridges into his palm to ascertain that none was a blank, reloaded, relocked, snapped open the safety, looked up at Croyd with the gun hanging in his right hand.

Croyd queried: "Familiar with it?"

"I played with one in a museum. Does it work?"

Beautifully. Why don't you try it?"

"On what or whom?"

"On me."

"Why?"

"Your doom-spume had disintegrated. Nevertheless, you want some sort of revenge. I am dispensable."

"*Can* you be killed, Croyd?"

"Your gun is loaded with explosive bullets. I can't be revived if I am smithereened."

"There has got to be some kind of catch. You say the gun works. Ah—are the cartridges charged?"

"Fully."

"When I fire the gun, it will explode in my hand and kill me."

"The gun will not explode. It will fire normally, and safely for you."

"Then—what catch? Oh: we're in nontime; I am synthesizing my breathing-air around me, but there is no air in the small sector of cartridge-ignition. Old-time explosives need oxygen to fire."

"Your scholarship glimmers there, Dino. The major component of the explosive charge is potassium nitrate which supplies the oxygen for the detonating drive of the bullet. In short, the cartridge has its self-contained oxygen supply. Believe me: the gun will fire kill-Croyd bullets."

Frowning, Dino again examined the gun. He queried: "Why does the great Croyd place himself at mortal risk?"

"Because I do not believe that you will shoot me."

"Why?"

"Because if I am dead, you will not have me around to hate."

"May I—test the gun first?"

"You have six shots. Save at least one for me."

"A test target?"

"We're in nontime. Here, you can mentally synthesize one."

After pause for thought, Dino half-turned and pointed to a nonlocus in the nonsky out beyond the rail. A ring-target materialized there. Taking aim with one perfectly rigid arm, he squeezed the trigger. A small hole appeared in the bullseye, but there was no noise, for there is no sound-mediating atmosphere in nontime—which reminded Dino that his current converse with Croyd must, after all, be mental.

He fired three more times at the target. All holes were in the bullseye: only three tightly-patterned holes, but one was wider than the others.

Croyd remarked: "Pray save the remaining two. If your first shot should fail to kill me, I'd appreciate a coup de grâce."

Dino, in profound trouble, turned to his mentor. "Croyd, I've made an ass of myself; but we can't brush it off so easily, because only brilliant intervention prevented me from annihilating three or maybe four galaxies. And now something is telling me that my hatred of you is frivolous. Nevertheless, Croyd, I continue to hate you. Why is that?"

Said Croyd: "You have the gun—and two remaining rounds."

Snake-strike Trigg jammed the gun-muzzle into his own mouth and fired.

brief anguish

whereafter, painlessly awkward feeling of own head splitting open and brains exploding out

a scene from which Dino gently drifted backward-upward (but not too far away) and hovered helplessly perceiving the dramatics on the breeze-way-bridge.

where the Trigg-body, eyes glazed and wide, let his gun hang in his right hand, trying with his left to palpate his permanently ruined skull, then let drop his left and shoved the gun again into his mouth and fired again but nothing further happened to him because he was already ruined.

In the impotently soul-anguished overviewing of double-Dino, the Trigg-body's open-blasted head came up and he stared wildly at Croyd—who observed, almost tenderly: "Yes indeed, my dear Dino: either shot would certainly have killed you—had you been alive. Happily, your body and its bloody brains are astral rather than physical: your magnificent jet-spume absolutely murdered you."

20. The Judging of Dino

Dino lowered eyes, and he was suffering, not from fear, but because he felt that it would be impossible to punish him adequately.

At first in him there was dullness, then wonder, then vast amazement when he heard Tannen inquire: "Tell me, good Dino—what judgment would *you* consider just?"

Up came Dino's head, very slowly. "*Good* Dino?" he ejaculated. He felt himself dissolving in the profound eyes of now-visible Tannen; and he felt the steady gaze of Croyd upon him.

Dino studied the question, scanning for possible retrieval of an idea all the vastness of his mindsoul.

With his nontongue he nonwet his nonlips. Tannen waited. Croyd watched.

Shakily, but with determination, Dino deposed: "Hell."

Up went a Tannen-brow, and the President's mouth twitched. "One is not being profane?"

"Not at all. You asked me a question. Hell is my answer."

"You would have me send you Hellward?"

"I deserve the absolute worst. I *want* to be punished by the absolute worst. Is not Hell the absolute worst?"

"Hell, for a mindsoul like yourself, would consist in hanging forever helpless in featureless nontime compulsively uphill-rolling the rock of your guilt."

"I will take it."

"—Knowing at every noninstant of eternity that you will *never* be free of this compulsion, that you will *never* regain any control at all, that the self-laceration of it will *never* be dulled."

"I accept it. I *beg* for it!"

"Bit of a waste, don't you think?"

Dino, after hesitation, blinked and queried: "I beg your pardon?"

"Croyd, tell him what I mean."

Promptly said Croyd: "He means, good friend Dino, that your cosmic adventure may have cleansed you of all your compulsions, leaving your marvelous mind free to swing loose, at last, in the process of dreaming great dreams and finding means to make them real. To be sure, you did nearly annihilate several galaxies; on the other hand, as a classical Freudian error, you brought aboard ship a double device for canceling-out your own doom-spume—"

"I did *what?*"

"You didn't need Musician Frey aboard, you didn't need that ultrasynthesizer aboard: the Zauberger flakes would have done the job."

"Are you suggesting that I *wanted* my diabolism to be canceled-out?"

"Not consciously so, but way down deep in. Remember that Trigg *never* made mistakes: perfect control, remember? and since Trigg this time *did* make just those mistakes, and consequently for the first time lost control, clearly the actions of Serpent Trigg were speaking with a forked tongue.

"No, don't argue any further. We're talking all around the central point, which is, that no matter how many people and civilizations and natural environments you *might* have slain in the course of your silly vendetta, still your mind is cleansed and freed, and it now can be powerfully creative in the service of the ultrasynthesis. That you *may* have purged your soul, your intimate-inward self, came clear to me when you sighed with honest relief at your jet's neutralizing, when you shot yourself instead of Croyd, and finally, having heard Hell thoroughly defined for you, when you opted for Hell.

"Tannen—otherwise Osiris, lord of judgment but also lord of physical and psychic fertility—I have now a compound judgment to recommend, subject to Dino's consent. It is, first, that you rule out Hell as a possibility for Dino. Then second, it is that you consign Dino to me."

"It is so ruled, Croyd Thoth," quietly declared Tannen. "Dino Trigg—is it to be Croyd?"

In the quietude of ultimate blessing, Dino responded without any quaver at all: "Great Judge, for me to be once again a creature of Croyd is an exquisitely refined form of Hell. Indeed—Croyd!"

Whereat both Tannen and Croyd vanished in a swirling of nonfog. Enveloped therein, Dino nonheard a well-known mind-voice: *The if-nodes in uptime are usable in a number of ways. One can recreate a very complex past situation and inject a germinal mind back into its old body track in that situation, to learn whether this time he will make the same old choices at his choice-points. Want to try it, Dino? Win or lose?"*

"Having gone through all this," Trigg retorted, "I am sure to do it differently."

Doesn't follow. You see—you will be deprived of your recent memory; it will all seem new to you.

Baffled, Dino demanded: "Then how can I fail to make all the same mistakes?"

I said that your inward attitudes appear to have been changed by the experience. They may produce change.

"And if they do?"

Then you will have released yourself from karma.
"And if I fail?"
If you fail, you fall back into the same old cycle, over and over again, including your defeat, over and over again. Only, during your eternal recycling, you will remember, and remember, and remember. I think you recently remarked that this would be Hell?

The austerely functional board room was ovoid. Seated people were arranged along both side walls, one parenthesis open-facing the other. Between them, a broad space of floor was empty; but by crouching and peering upward, Kolly could see a large device hanging above and presumably lowerable.

Chairman Croyd was seated behind a small desk at the center of one parenthesis of small desks facing the board. He was flanked by the ten ministers who were his top officers in Galactic.

Trigg sat at Croyd's immediate right, being first among these ministers. He was smilingly relaxed at the moment, but poised for electrical deployment. Croyd—recalling (as Dino did not) all that had transpired the first time around—prickled with apprehension.)

Croyd and his battery of ministers were gazing somewhat upward at a toward-them-open, daised counter-parenthesis: a broad semi-circular high-polished ebonoid table behind whose convex edge were nine swiveling easy chairs eight of which were occupied (Croyd having vacated his own center chair for this quintennial occasion).

Behind and above the board-arc sat President Tannen: he, too, remembered and was apprehensive.

Tannen spoke now, easily despite unease. "Hearing no objection, I will proceed to the prime business. Chairman Croyd, are you standing for reelection?" Croyd stood, assented, sat. "Prior to discussion by this board, do you wish to enter any remarks?" Croyd replied, holding his middle-baritone voice in restraint: "Not prior to discussion, sir."

Tannen queried: "Does anyone wish to arise as a competing candidate for the chair?"

Dino Trigg stood: hair and trim beard golden blond, eyes a surprising dark brown, handsome-flexible-potent. His generally unexpected self-presentation startled and even shocked his fellow ministers and some board members.

Inquired unrufflable Tannen: "First Minister Trigg, you are challenging Chairman Croyd for the chair of this board?"

Dino opened mouth to speak, then hesitated. Croyd and Tannen were rigid: it was the if-node, the choice point . . .

Dino's mouth-corners quirked up; he spread hands; whimsically he remarked, "I beg the President's pardon; I am all full of something that I wished to report about stellar jets, momentarily I lost track of these proceedings, this is not the time—"

Dino sat down, and he was smiling serenely for the first time in years.

Board-members, ministers, and all the scene flickered and vanished.

Out of nonspace came Croyd's voice: "You have passed, Minister Trigg. Unhappily, all the galaxy remembers your former rebellion in this board room. But luckily, only a few of us will ever remember about Schnarliwarli. This frees the creativity of Tannen and me to paint an ameliorating picture during perhaps a two-year period of Trigg-absence.

"What would you think, Dino, of a hitch as Galactic Ambassador to Hudibras?"

DAW

NEW DIMENSIONS IN MILITARY SF

Charles Ingrid
THE SAND WARS
He was a soldier fighting against both mankind's alien foe and the evil at the heart of the human Dominion Empire, trapped in an alien-altered suit of armor which, if worn too long, could transform him into a sand warrior—a no-longer human berserker.

☐ SOLAR KILL (Book 1)	(UE2209—$3.50)
☐ LASERTOWN BLUES (Book 2)	(UE2260—$3.50)
☐ CELESTIAL HIT LIST (Book 3)	(UE2306—$3.50)
☐ ALIEN SALUTE (Book 4)	(UE2329—$3.95)

W. Michael Gear
THE SPIDER TRILOGY
The Prophets of the lost colony planet called World could see the many pathways of the future, and when the conquering Patrol Ships of the galaxy-spanning Directorate arrived, they found the warriors of World ready, armed and waiting.

☐ THE WARRIORS OF SPIDER (Book 1)	(UE2287—$3.95)
☐ THE WAY OF SPIDER (Book 2)	(UE2318—$3.95)

John Steakley
☐ ARMOR
Impervious body armor had been devised for the commando forces who were to be dropped onto the poisonous surface of A-9, the home world of mankind's most implacable enemy. But what of the man inside the armor? This tale of cosmic combat will stand against the best of Gordon Dickson or Poul Anderson.
(UE2368—$4.50)
